**"It seems that [...]
me on, Amy H[...]**

Amy could hardly believe what Jack was saying. "You mean," she said unsteadily, "that all this time, you've—"

"Wanted to hold you, run my hands all over your body. Yes, Amy. I've dreamed of taking off every stitch of your clothes and kissing you everywhere."

Overcome by her own desire for him, she could barely speak. "I didn't know."

"Now you do," Jack replied. "I want so much to love you."

She shivered at the caressing warmth of his magic voice. "Jack, if you're my friend, you won't do this."

His thumb traced the fullness of her bottom lip, and then he covered her mouth with his and wrapped her in his arms. Raising his head for a moment, he whispered, "Haven't you realized? Our friendship is over, Amy."

To my sister Becca,
an independent thinker
and the best dancer in the family.

———— 🍎 ————

VICKI LEWIS THOMPSON
is also the author of
these novels in
Temptation

MINGLED HEARTS
PROMISE ME SUNSHINE
AN IMPRACTICAL PASSION
THE FIX-IT MAN
AS TIME GOES BY
CUPID'S CAPER

The Flip Side

VICKI LEWIS THOMPSON

MILLS & BOON LIMITED
ETON HOUSE, 18–24 PARADISE ROAD
RICHMOND, SURREY TW9 1SR

First published in Great Britain 1989 by
Mills & Boon Limited, Eton House, 18–24 Paradise Road,
Richmond, Surrey, TW9 1SR

© Vicki Lewis Thompson 1987

ISBN 0 263 76459 1

21–8903

Made and printed in Great Britain

1

"*THIS IS JACK 'HULA HIPS' BOND coming to you live from beautiful downtown Bellingham, Washington, otherwise known as K-Playland. And don't forget; tomorrow's the big day. KPLY's hula contest happens at the Cascade Mall. We've got ten finalists who will be swiveling and swaying for the cause.*"

Amy spread another cracker with Cheez Whiz and smiled in the direction of her four portable radios, all of which were blaring. "Jack, my boy, I've been practicing all week."

"*And the winner will jet to Hawaii, with a traveling companion of his or her choice. My cousin Ernie has volunteered to go if a woman wins. Don't take him, girls. He's not much of a world traveler. Ernie's the kind of guy who will call room service and order a peanut butter sandwich. To go.*"

Amy laughed. Jack had created Cousin Ernie a couple of years ago to beef up the show. Amy had always wondered if Cousin Ernie took the place of the brothers and sisters Jack used to wish for. She and Brad were the closest thing he'd ever had to siblings. Amy lifted her cracker in salute. "Here's to you, Jack Blickensderfer, and the good times we've shared. May tomorrow be another one." This time, she'd get to Hawaii.

BY THREE the following afternoon, Amy knew exactly why people in western Washington didn't run around in grass skirts and bikinis in November. What dingledorf had planned this as an outside event? She might not dance the best hula in the contest, but it was guaranteed to be the liveliest.

A chill wind pushed threatening clouds toward Bellingham from the direction of the bay. By that night Mount Baker would have more snow piled on its craggy peaks. Amy shivered and looked around at her fellow contestants. Nobody had dressed as scantily as she.

Both men who had made the finals wore jeans, although one had pulled a pair of Hawaiian print shorts over them and tied a string of beer cans around his waist. A necklace of church keys formed his lei, and his shirt was stenciled with the slogan Belling—Ham. He'd be a crowd-pleaser, Amy decided.

All the women were pretty well covered up, too. One had on a jogging suit with a little grass skirt over it, and another dashed to her car and came back with a ski jacket, which she zipped up against the cold wind. Amy's coat was in her car, too, but she vowed not to get it and ruin all her efforts to look authentic.

Jack's entrance befitted his position as the celebrity of the hour. He drove his black IROC-Z Camaro up to the grandstand with a flourish.

Amy was impressed with the enthusiastic reception given him by a group of teenagers near the grandstand. Jack Bond really did have a following. Nevertheless, she had a bone to pick with the great deejay.

He emerged from the car and vaulted to the platform, right in front of her. "Well, look at this," he said with a grin. "If it isn't Amy Hobson goes Hawaiian. I noticed your name on the list of final contestants."

She looked him over from his scuffed Reeboks and the white suspenders holding up his 501 Levi's jeans to his red sweatshirt with the KPLY logo on the front. He was dressed for cold weather, the rat. "Jack Blickensderfer, are you the one responsible for holding this farce in the parking lot instead of inside the nice warm mall?"

"Shh." He put a finger to his lips. "What if one of my loyal fans hears you call me that? Me, the great Jack Bond, keeper of the airwaves?"

"Are you the one or not?"

"Yes, ma'am. The parking lot holds more people than the mall, and I wanted lots of people."

"When I get pneumonia I plan to sue."

"You should have worn a leotard and tights or something under this deal."

"But then I wouldn't look Hawaiian."

Jack nodded. "What you look is blue. Didn't Elvis Presley do a song about that? 'You and me, and Blue Hawaii.'"

"You're in deep shinola, Jack, my friend."

"Wouldn't be the first time. Well, gotta go. Wouldn't want anyone to think I'm prejudiced in favor of one of the contestants."

"Good old honest Jack."

"Yep." He turned and jogged over to the microphone.

"That's you, all right," Amy said to herself, watching him pick up the hand mike and address the audience and contestants with practiced ease. In spite of her irritation, she had to admit to herself that she felt a certain pride because she knew this man in the spotlight today. With his dark curly hair and black-fringed blue eyes, he probably had all the young girls swooning over him.

But he was just plain old Jack to her, the boy who'd spent almost as much time at the Hobson house as her brother. Jack was the boy with grease-stained T-shirts who used to work on cars with Brad and play basketball in the driveway until they were both soaked in sweat. Sometimes Amy had played, too.

"I hope all of you brought your spare change," Jack said to the crowd. "During the dance contest my KPLY helpers will pass among you with cans like this." He held up a slotted container. "Be generous. We're halfway to our goal. We're hoping to build the teen reading center next year, with your help."

Amy had forgotten about the reading center, but it was typical of Jack to be involved in some cause or other. This year it was illiteracy among teenagers. She remembered that her entry fee in the contest had been a tax-deductible donation.

Jack turned from the crowd to the ten people standing on the platform with him. "Okay, you hula maniacs. When the music begins, I want all of you to begin dancing. The good people out here will choose the top five contestants, and I'll make the final selection. Personally." He lifted his eyebrows and hoots went up from the audience. "And if one of the two guys up here is the best dancer, he'll win the trip." More hoots. "Would Jack Bond lie?"

"Like a rug!" shouted a man in the audience.

"Well, it's partly up to you folks. If you don't include any men in the final five, I can't prove what an impartial judge I am. So let's see how you do." He switched off the mike and turned on the gentle strains of "Pearly Shells."

The man with the beer cans around his waist clattered around his portion of the stage in a frenzied motion that had nothing to do with the music. But the rest of the contestants tried to dance their best version of a hula.

Amy swayed rhythmically to the song. Thank God she'd been a pompon girl in high school and was used to performing in front of an audience. With her limited peripheral vision she could see that several of the other dancers weren't. They had no stage presence and little sense of rhythm. But one woman was different. Amy picked her out immediately as the dancer to beat.

Jack walked up and down the line of gyrating bodies and winked at Amy when he passed. The gesture was deliberately lighthearted, but Jack wasn't fooling himself. He was damned worried.

Last week, when Amy's name had been drawn as one of the ten finalists, he'd been amused. It hadn't really occurred to him that she might be good enough to win. After all, she'd always been like a kid sister to him. Kid sisters didn't dance the hula like this, did they?

Covertly he watched her sensuous movements in the grass skirt. Lord almighty. Amy Hobson had breasts, and curving hips and shapely legs. He felt almost incestuous for thinking so, and he tried vainly to control his thoughts. She'd inherited her mother's dark hair and brown eyes, and with that white flower tucked behind her ear, she looked Hawaiian, which translated quickly in Jack's mind to sexy and exotic.

He'd lost track of her after Brad's wedding, except that he knew she wasn't living at home anymore and he remembered his mother saying that Amy worked as a secretary for Bateman's lumberyard. He'd considered it a waste of a sharp mind, but Amy had always been like that, making mediocre grades in school when she could have been valedictorian of her class.

And now here she was, undulating on this open-air stage with practically no clothes on. His first impulse when he saw her from a distance was to rush up and throw a blanket over her. Fortunately for both of them, he realized in time that he had no right to do that. Instead he'd fallen into the old pattern of joking around with her.

Apparently she hadn't noticed anything amiss with him, because she'd acted like the old Amy he used to know, feisty as hell. But in that outfit, and dancing the hula, she wasn't the old Amy. No matter how severely Jack lectured himself, he formed increasingly indecent pictures in his mind as he watched her move. He hoped the crowd vote would eliminate her from the running.

It didn't. The crazy guy with the beer cans made the finals, along with four women. Amy was one of them. Jack prayed to the gods of fairness that he would be able to make an unbiased decision.

The second Hawaiian tune he'd selected had no lyrics and a faster pace. He'd planned the sequence to separate the real dancers from the ones who could manage a slow, undemanding beat. The beer-can fellow, who might have been tipping a few before the contest, dropped out halfway through the song and sat on the edge of the grandstand, puffing. Of the four remaining, two stood out from the rest, and again, one of them was Amy.

This time when Jack walked past her he didn't wink. It took all his presence of mind to look noncommittal and calm while he watched her hips shimmy in perfect time to the beat. Where had she learned how to do that?

He forced himself to concentrate on the other strong contender, a blond woman in her mid-thirties. She wore a sarong and a flesh-colored bodysuit underneath it. And she was good. For pure technique she was a better dancer than Amy, but she didn't affect his hormones the way Amy did.

The music continued interminably. He'd chosen a long number on purpose, knowing most of the crowd came to see people performing a sexy hula. His palms began to sweat. All his instincts told him to give the grand prize to Amy. Her dancing was good, and her freshness made her movements even more provocative.

But dammit to hell, he was prejudiced. He hated admitting it to himself. How would someone else, someone who didn't know Amy at all, view this contest?

The blond woman was excellent and showed a sophistication that Amy lacked. Of course, that was the very thing he preferred about Amy's dancing. Jack wished he'd never dreamed up this stupid contest. He wished he could go home.

After a drumroll, the music stopped. Without looking at any of the contestants, Jack slowly walked back to the microphone. He turned on the switch.

"Ladies and—" He paused to clear his throat, something he almost never had to do when he spoke into a mike. He'd always been a natural speaker. But he felt as if someone had a stranglehold on his vocal cords.

"Ladies and gentlemen. I will now announce the winners."

Total silence settled over the crowd.

"Cousin Ernie wanted to be here today to hand out the prizes, but last night his cat knocked over his ant farm and the little devils crawled right into his underwear drawer. The last I saw of Ernie he was hightailing it up to Mount Baker to sit in the snow."

The crowd laughed.

"So I'll have to do this by myself," Jack continued. "Starting with the fifth runner-up. I guess we all know who this is."

The man with the beer cans stood up and raised his hands above his head in acknowledgment of the crowd's cheers.

"Randy Slocum receives a very generous gift certificate from the Sound and Fury Record Shop." Jack paused for the clapping to die down. "Sound and Fury certainly describes your dancing technique, Randy."

The man accepted his gift certificate with a deep bow and almost fell off the stage amid more laughter and applause.

Jack held up his hand. "Fourth runner-up who will receive dinner for two at Alfredo's is Joyce Danner." He handed the gift certificate to a freckled redhead as the crowd voiced its approval. "Third runner-up and winner of a new fall coat from Benson's is Geri Clay."

Jack waited for the applause to cease before he spoke again. "Of course, when I announce the second runner-up, you will know who won the all-expenses-paid, four-day trip for two to Hawaii. The second runner-up will receive a Cuisinart food processor from The Cookery."

Amy held her breath. This could be it, her big victory at last. This trip was so very important to her, to her parents. She'd danced well, and Jack was her friend, after all. If she was equal to the blond woman, shouldn't Jack choose a friend over a stranger?

"My choice wasn't easy. I want all you guys out there to know that judging this contest was a tough job, but somebody had to do it."

Several people hooted their disbelief.

"No, really. I think you'll agree that both of these ladies know their way around a hula."

The crowd whistled and clapped in response.

"Good luck, sweetheart," said the woman next to Amy under cover of the crowd noise. "Have you ever been to Hawaii?"

"No. Have you?"

"Five times. That's where I learned to dance."

Amy wanted to throttle the woman. How unfair if she should win, after her five trips to Amy's none!

"But choose I must," Jack continued. "So without further ado, our second runner-up is—" Jack paused.

Amy clenched her teeth and closed her eyes.

"Amy Hobson. Evelyn Saint wins the trip!"

Amy didn't open her eyes. She'd lost. So close, and she'd lost. Damn Jack Blickensderfer! How could he do this to her? The applause and cheers for Evelyn Saint drowned out her muttered curse as she glared at Jack. He was hugging that woman!

"Whew," Jack said into the mike. "Gratitude is such fun. Anyway, I'd like all five winners to please stay for pictures. Randy, can you stand up a little longer, buddy?"

Amy smiled stoically through the photography session and even managed a few curt words of congratulation to Evelyn Saint. But when the picture-taking was finally over, Amy headed for the steps leading off the stage.

"Amy."

She turned as someone grasped her arm.

"Hey, I'm sorry, kid."

She glanced up at Jack. "Not as sorry as I am."

"Was it so important, this trip?" His brow wrinkled in concern.

"More important than you could ever guess," she said, and wrenched away from him.

Amy stormed off the platform and ran to her car, in her anger enjoying the bite of the cold asphalt on her bare feet. This was the best chance she'd ever had to get to Hawaii, and Jack Blickensderfer had ruined it. After all the years she'd been so sweet to him, he had picked this moment to turn into a gold-plated ass.

She should have told her mother years ago about the hidden stack of girlie magazines that belonged to Jack and Brad. She should have kicked Jack where it hurt when they played basketball. Instead of handing him a wrench when he was working on Brad's car, she should have dropped it on his foot. He was scum. He was dirt. Lowest of the low. Vilest of the vile.

She drove home in a rage and flung open the door to her apartment. The phone was ringing. She let it ring. Whoever was calling wouldn't want to talk to her now.

She ripped off the grass skirt that she'd spent hours making by cutting green plastic trash bags into strips. Her lei, created from dime-store silk flowers, joined the grass skirt in the garbage can, and the white gardenia sailed in after that.

Clad only in her bikini, Amy ran into the bedroom, grabbed her quilted bedspread and wrapped herself in a cocoon of misery before settling into the corner of the couch for a good cry.

But crying was a boring activity, and she soon gave it up. What she longed for was a dart board with Jack's picture on it. Amy sighed. Maybe the blond woman was a better dancer. After all, she'd learned the movements in Hawaii, while Amy's training came from community school classes. Jack must have thought the blond woman was a better dancer. Because Jack was a very honest person. Too damned honest to suit Amy's tastes.

Deep down she knew she couldn't put all the blame on Jack. He'd made the best decision he knew how. But at that moment, Amy found great satisfaction in heaping all her frustration on Jack Blickensderfer's broad shoulders. He could have been such a hero. Instead he was such a heel.

The phone rang again, and she reached for it this time. Maybe some company would help her crummy mood.

"Amy?"

"Tell me this isn't who I think it is."

"You forgot your food processor."

"Put it where the sun don't shine, Jack."

"You think I liked the job of choosing between two very good dancers, one of whom I've known forever? I wanted to disqualify myself, but it was too late."

"She's been to Hawaii five times." Amy began to sniffle again and wiped her nose on the edge of her quilt.

"I know. She told me. Look, I realize you're upset and think you should have won. Maybe you should have."

"What? You mean there was some *doubt* in your mind, and you still picked her?"

"She was good. And I was afraid knowing you was making me biased in your favor, so—"

"So you leaned over backward to be fair! Thanks a whole hell of a lot, Jack! Do you have any idea how much this trip means to me?"

"From the volume of your voice, I'm beginning to find out. Listen, do you want this food processor or don't you?"

"No. I process food as little as possible."

"Still not domesticated, are you?"

"I don't need this abuse, Jack."

"Well, if you don't want the food machine, maybe I'll give it to my mother."

"The hell you will. I'll give it to *my* mother."

"Your language is the pits, Amy. Then you want your prize?"

"I guess. I did win the thing." Amy sighed. "I'll pick it up from the station."

"If you'll promise not to throw rocks at me, I'll bring it by when I get off tonight at ten. If you'll be home, that is."

"Where would I be? Out celebrating my good fortune in winning a food processor?"

"Amy, this is a very nice prize. It's not my fault you're not into kitchen gadgets. Should I bring this over tonight or not?"

"Better that you make a trip than me, I guess."

"You're so gracious. Is this your address on the entry blank, in the Bayview Apartments?"

"That's it."

"And do you have one?"

"One what?"

"A view of the bay."

"Hah. Not on my salary, Jack. I'm on the ground floor."

"Okay. See you about ten-fifteen."

Amy hung up the phone with another sigh. A food processor. Her mother would be thrilled, even if Amy wasn't. The contest wasn't a total loss, she decided.

By nine-thirty she wished Jack wasn't coming. The apartment felt drafty, and she wanted to put on her flannel nightgown and snuggle into bed. Instead she switched on her radios. Not that she particularly wanted to hear Jack's voice. He just happened to play her kind of music.

Rummaging in the bathroom cabinet, Amy pulled out her manicure supplies and carried them to her favorite grooming spot at the kitchen table. Maybe a change of color on her fingernails would give her a lift.

Methodically she removed the dark magenta shade from each nail. She'd hoped the exotic polish would draw attention to the graceful movements of her hands during the hula. So much for that strategy.

The music ended and Jack's soothing baritone filled the small apartment. *"Here's hoping everyone out in Playland is cuddling with someone special on this blustery Saturday night."*

Amy wondered idly if Jack had a girlfriend. When she knew him before he'd had a couple of very serious relationships, but as far as she knew he'd never married anyone.

"Hey, how about that hula contest today? We warmed up the Cascade Mall parking lot this afternoon, and if you weren't there, you missed some intense dancing. Maybe not as intense as Cousin Ernie's after his ant farm showed up in his underwear drawer, but lively, nevertheless...."

Amy grimaced at the reminder of the miserable contest.

"We have our winner, Evelyn Saint, who will soon wing her way to Hawaii. Our sponsors for that trip were the good people at First Class Travel. Call them before you make those winter vacation plans."

"Sure thing, Jack." Amy smoothed a coat of strawberry polish on her thumbnail. "You dork." But her anger had lost its punch. She'd always been lousy at holding a grudge.

By the time Jack signed off at ten, her nails were a bright cheerful pink and Amy was almost looking forward to his visit. They hadn't talked in ages. Of course, maybe Jack hadn't planned to stay for any length of time. The thought deflated her spirits a little.

But when she opened her door to a broad grin and the aroma of pizza, Amy knew Jack was staying.

"I hope you have beer," he said over the two boxes in his arms.

She peered past him to the shiny car parked by the curb. "That really is your Camaro."

"Mine and the bank's. It's the only luxury item I own, or own part of, anyway."

"You always were a little crazy when it came to cars. Let me amend that. You always were a little crazy, period." Amy took the flat box on top and sniffed. "Canadian bacon and green pepper?"

"That better still be your favorite."

"I'm impressed that you remembered."

"After all the nights you blackmailed Brad and me into buying it for you? Fat chance I'd forget. Where do you want this food grinder thing?"

"Anywhere. On the couch."

Jack plopped the box down, took off his coat and threw it across the large carton. Then he glanced around the room. "Amy, why do you have four radios and two teeny television sets? You're not a fence for some ring of thieves, are you?"

She put the pizza box on the kitchen table and opened the refrigerator. "Thanks a lot. You always did suspect the worst of me, Jack."

"A few years ago that was the wise way to operate. Brad and I worked very effectively from that premise. We despaired of raising you, Amy Lorraine."

"Drink your beer and be quiet." She grinned and handed him a chilled bottle. Having Jack around again was fun.

"Löwenbräu? Did you run out and buy this because I was coming?"

"What an egomaniac. I happen to like it, too."

"What good taste you have." He winked at her. "Come on," he added, gesturing toward the table with the bottle, "your pizza's getting cold."

"Boy, does this bring back memories," Amy said, sitting across from him and opening the pizza box. "I'm sorry Brad isn't here."

"Me too." Jack pulled a wedge of pizza, trailing strings of melted cheese, from the box.

"And you got extra cheese."

"Of course." He bit into the warm crust and closed his eyes. "Mm-mm."

Amy stared at his long black lashes for a moment before taking her own slice of pizza. She'd forgotten how long those lashes were. She'd always been envious.

The pizza tasted perfect on this chilly night, and she gave a little sigh of satisfaction. Jack was a pretty good guy, after all.

He polished off his first piece and picked up a second. "So where *did* the radios and televisions come from?"

"Contests."

"You won them?"

"Not on purpose. Each time I was trying for the Hawaiian trip. In the process I got radios, two televisions, plus a lot of other junk I won't mention. Oh, and at least a year's supply of Cheez Whiz."

Jack's blue eyes twinkled with amusement. "Maybe I should have brought crackers instead of pizza."

"Don't be smart."

"What's with this Hawaii bit, Amy? Some new obsession of yours?"

She studied him carefully, unsure of how much to say. "It has to do with Mom and Dad."

Jack looked crestfallen. "Aw, Amy. You wanted to win the trip for them. God, I should have known. I feel like a real jerk."

He looked so miserable that she took pity on him. "Don't blame yourself. Besides, it's more complicated than that. I wouldn't have given them the trip. I would have gone."

"You would? I don't understand."

"I, uh, have to go over and inspect some property I'm buying."

"Buying..." With a dazed expression he looked around the rented apartment with its inexpensive furniture.

"I can tell what you're thinking, Jack. I don't look rich enough to be buying Hawaiian property. And I'm not. But you see, Mom and Dad..." She stopped speaking. No one knew of her plan. Why was she about to tell everything to Jack?

"That's right. They always talked about retiring in Hawaii." He stared at her. "But you said that you were buying it."

"I—I am."

"Why? Haven't they been saving for years? I remember Brad telling me that they had a nice nest egg tucked away."

Amy shook her head. "Not anymore."

"What do you mean?"

"The money's gone," she said bitterly. "And it's all my fault."

2

"WHAT?" Jack frowned in confusion. "Amy, are we talking about thousands of dollars?"

She nodded.

"How could you lose—"

"A bad investment." She dropped her gaze. "I was engaged to a man who promised to double their money, make their dream come true that much sooner. He was a fraud."

"Oh, Amy. You poor kid."

She glanced up, and her eyes were moist. "You used to tell me I was too gullible for my own good."

"Did you give him money, too?"

"A little." She laughed. "There wasn't much to give, fortunately. I've never been a saver. But Mom and Dad were a different story. I . . . guess he became engaged to me in order to win their confidence and get their money."

Jack uttered an oath under his breath. "But can't you prosecute? Make him pay it back?"

Amy shook her head. "By the time we figured out the situation, there was no money left. He'd spent it on high living and then declared bankruptcy. He's doing time in prison, but that doesn't help my folks much. Anyway, I understand lots of people in Seattle lost more than we did."

"What a rotten thing to have happen." Jack took a swig of his beer. "I don't know which is worse, the emotional hurt you suffered or the financial loss your folks had. I wouldn't blame you if you'd sworn off men altogether."

"I almost have. Of course I schedule these talks with myself about the fact that not all men are like Philip."

"Send all your dates over to me from now on, Amy. I'll check them out right quick."

She smiled at him. "You and Brad tried that in high school. I didn't like it then, either."

"And what happened? Every time you went against our advice you ended up with a loser."

"Maybe that's why this bothers me so much." Amy stared at the half-eaten pizza. "Apparently my judgment hasn't improved."

"Love does weird things to our heads, Amy," he said softly. "Don't be so hard on yourself. You've had a rough time."

Amy's hand tightened into a fist. "My folks have had a rougher time, and they don't deserve that. But I'm determined to make everything right again. I'm buying this property for them, and Dad has his disability from the navy. I'll figure out a way for them to retire in Hawaii yet."

"I don't see this as entirely your responsibility, Amy."

"I do. Mom and Dad wouldn't have invested their money if I hadn't said it was a good idea. Since Brad left, they've depended on me for advice about most of their major decisions. But this was one time they should have asked someone else."

"Does Brad know?"

"He doesn't, and you'd better not tell him, Jack Blickensderfer!"

"But he's doing pretty well, isn't he? The last letter I got said something about a promotion. He could help you with—"

"No!"

"Amy, you—"

"I don't want Brad to know about this, at least until I've fixed it up. Can't you understand, Jack? Brad always thinks of me as his screw-up little sister. If he has to bail me out of this one, I'll never have his respect. Or Mom and Dad's."

"Brad thinks the world of you. So do your parents, Amy."

"They don't put me in the same class with Brad, I can tell you that. He was the good student, the one who went to college, the one who got the exciting job in Spokane. Mom and Dad think he hung the moon. I can't have them thanking him for straightening out the big mess Amy got them into. I just can't."

Jack covered her clenched fist with his hand. "Okay. I understand. And I won't tell Brad if that's what you want."

"It is. I...I probably shouldn't have told you, but this whole thing has been weighing on my mind, and you're like a member of the family, I guess."

He looked into her troubled brown eyes and tried to recall the days when he'd thought of her as a sister. Those days seemed so far away now, and her hand beneath his was so soft, her parted lips so inviting. Years ago he'd been the one who helped her out of many teenage scrapes. But she wasn't a teenager anymore.

Amy smiled. "With you around, I always felt I had two big brothers."

Abruptly he removed his hand and grabbed for his beer. "Yep," he said gruffly. "That's right, two brothers."

"You don't sound happy about it."

"Believe me, I was. I practically lived at your house for a while. Your mom and dad were super to me when I was going through my parents' divorce. Your family was my haven." He gulped the rest of his beer.

Amy found his mood change confusing. "I heard your mother and stepfather moved away," she ventured.

"Right after I graduated from high school. I should be grateful they waited until then. They're very happy, it seems, living in L.A. I rarely see them."

"And your dad?"

"I get a postcard once in a while from whatever country he's filming in."

"I've seen some of his documentaries on TV, Jack. They're good."

"Yeah." He reached for another piece of pizza. "Got another beer?"

"Sure." As she walked to the refrigerator, Amy searched for a way to dispel the gloom from his mood. "Remember the time you and Brad took me to that war movie, and the two of you decided to crawl down the aisle on your bellies and see if anyone noticed?"

Jack munched on his pizza and smiled. "And you crawled right after us and ruined your new white dress. We never imagined you'd try to follow us in that dress. You didn't squeal on us, either."

"I never squealed. About anything." She set the beer in front of him.

"Maybe not, but you sure threatened. Remember blackmailing us about our collection of *Playboy* magazines? I thought for sure you'd blow the whistle on us for those."

"Well, I didn't," she said, sitting down across from him once more, "but for a little while this afternoon I sure wished that I had. I was furious with you, Jack."

"I'll bet. I'd like to turn the clock back a few hours and make that decision over again."

Amy sighed. "I really want to get a look at that property. The company that sold it to me made the place sound wonderful, but the more I think about it, the more I want to see for myself."

"How did you happen to buy it?"

"One of those deals where you get a free dinner and they make a sales pitch."

"That sounds a little risky, kiddo."

"I know, but I checked them out with the Better Business Bureau." Amy decided against telling Jack that she'd made her inquiries after she'd bought the property, not before.

"That's no guarantee. The BBB will have a record if there have been complaints, but if the business is too new, the complaints may not have been filed yet."

"I know, so I called a few real estate companies," Amy announced proudly. "One of them had an office in Hawaii, and they assured me the land development is legitimate. But I still want to see the place for myself. My lot is on the ocean, and I know the size of it, but other than that the brochure isn't very specific about the view and the beach, and what sort of vegetation is there."

"On the ocean, huh? That sounds good."

"Oh, I'm sure it will be beautiful."

"I'm sure it will." He gazed at her without speaking for a long moment. "Can't you save enough to fly over on your own? Some times of the year the flights are pretty cheap."

"Not cheap enough. The land payments take all my spare cash."

"Oh."

Amy began to squirm, as she always had under the scrutiny of those clear blue eyes. "I know what you're thinking. That I never did have much sense, and now I'm off on another wild tangent, as always."

"No, I wasn't thinking that at all," he said quietly.

"Then what were you thinking?"

He glanced down at the beer bottle in his hand. "That you're a very unselfish person. That you've grown up a lot." When he looked back up, his expression was filled with encouragement. "You'll win a trip soon, Amy. I'll start watching for contests, too. I'll help you."

"I appreciate that." She smiled warmly. "Do you realize that you're the only person I know who's been to Hawaii? I still have that postcard you sent me when you were in port there."

"You saved a silly postcard?" The thought pleased him tremendously.

"Of course. My friends were so jealous. A postcard from a sailor! Hawaii has always seemed like paradise to me, probably because Dad talked about it so much. How could you come back here to live after that? Didn't you want to stay?"

"No. Hawaii's pretty, but it's not for everyone."

"Maybe not, but it's the place for Mom and Dad. And where they go, I'll probably go. They need someone to help them through little emergencies."

"Your dad's not any better?"

"Not really. Head injuries are tricky. Sometimes he seems mentally sharper than other times, but he forgets things, and can't concentrate on details. That's why I feel so terrible about the investment thing."

"And your mother?"

"She still thinks of herself as a Filipino, a foreigner, and Dad's her protector and hero, as he always has been. Even in his condition, she lets him handle all the finances, and he screws them up. Then she calls me. She continues to avoid any real responsibility."

"That puts quite a burden on you, doesn't it?"

"I don't mind. Besides, I like the idea of going to Hawaii. It sounds exciting to me."

"And you almost made it today. Damn. The minute I saw your name on the list of finalists I should have gotten another deejay to judge."

"And Evelyn Saint would have won, anyway. She's a good dancer, and I'm not really mad at you anymore. You did the right thing, and I'll win a contest eventually, like you said."

"You're a good sport, but I still feel like a rat."

"Don't. Tell me about this teen reading project instead. How did you get involved?"

"Beeper McGee."

Amy laughed. "Who?"

"Beeper's an original kind of guy. On teen dedication night I'd get these calls asking that records be dedicated from Beeper to Julie, or Beeper to Stephanie. Dozens of girls were mentioned, and the same person wasn't calling in, either. Finally I asked one of the callers about Beeper."

"And?"

"Beeper turns out to be a seventeen-year-old who runs what you might term an adolescent syndicate. They call him Beeper because he wears a pager at all times."

"You mean those things doctors clip on their belts?"

"Yep. Beeper's parents have money, which they give in obscene amounts to their son, and he uses it to hire everything done for him, including schoolwork."

"Amazing."

"I finally met Beeper by offering him a guest deejay spot on the show. That's when I discovered he can't read."

"Because he's never had to."

"Not until he was a guest deejay. He didn't realize reading was part of the job. The problem came when he loved his little stint so much that he decided radio is the occupation for him. Now I'm tutoring him on the sly." Jack glanced at Amy. "No one knows about it except you."

She held up one hand in solemn oath. "You can trust me with your secret if I can trust you with mine."

"That's a deal. Anyway, Beeper says there are lots of kids with reading problems, but once they're in high school they do everything possible to cover it up. Not being able to read is embarrassing to them."

"Then how will you get them to go to a clinic?"

"We won't call it a clinic, for one thing. We'll call it a club. And it won't be a silent, gloomy place. I want to put money into a good sound system, and we'll run a snack bar that will bring in some money. The reading materials will be there, but casually so. And the aides will be young, no older than me. I'll probably try to find people closer to your age."

She gave him a sardonic look. "You mean really young types?"

"You didn't look so young today, in that hula skirt. Did your mom and dad know you were performing out there like that?"

"I'm twenty-four, Jack. I hardly need their permission anymore."

"You hardly ever asked, even when you did need their permission. You always were headstrong, Amy."

"That's why I'll make it to Hawaii."

"I'm sure you will." He rolled the beer bottle between his palms and studied her. Then he seemed to mentally collect himself. "Guess I'd better go home. It's late."

Amy stood when he did. She was sorry to see him go. "Thanks for bringing over the food processor. And the pizza was great. We haven't talked like this in a long time, Jack."

"No, we sort of lost touch without old Brad to bring us together." He walked into the living room and picked up his coat. "You know you're welcome to come down to the station anytime," he said, sliding his arms into the coat sleeves.

"Thanks. I might do that." But she wondered on what pretext she would drop in on him. They had no definite link now, other than his nebulous offer to help her with contest entries. And she hated to see Jack disappear out of her life again. "If you need a good deal on lumber for your reading center, I'll see what I can do." She was grasping at straws, and she knew it.

He smiled. "I'll remember that."

"Jack?"

He turned, already halfway out the door. "Yes?"

"You said there were lots of kids in Beeper's situation."

"That's what he tells me."

"And the clinic, I mean 'club,' won't be finished for a while. What happens to those kids?"

Jack shrugged. "I don't know. Beeper's all I can handle on my own. I suppose they'll muddle along as usual."

"What if I helped you? I could tutor someone. I remember how rough school can be."

"That's very generous, Amy, but . . ."

She bristled at his hesitation. "I *do* know how to read."

"I know you do. That's not the problem. I found out about Beeper by accident. I'd have to go through him to find another candidate and also be careful that he didn't think I betrayed his confidence."

Amy examined one pink fingernail. "If you think I'd be a flop, just say so."

"No, that's not it at all. I just . . . Would you want a boy or girl?"

She looked up. "Does it matter? After being around you and Brad all my life, I could work with a boy as easily as a girl."

"Amy, some of those boys are—"

"Jack Blickensderfer, I used to date kids like that."

Jack shuddered. "How I remember."

"But I don't want to push you into this. Maybe we should forget the idea."

"No. I like it. The more I think about you tutoring someone, the more I think you'd do a terrific job. Let me see what I can find out."

"Great." She grinned up at him as the cold draft from the door ruffled her dark hair.

"You realize this is strictly volunteer. Even though Beeper's loaded, he's not paying me anything."

Her grin faded. "I understand," she said stiffly. "You aren't the only one in the world who can be altruistic, you know."

"I know. Look what you're doing for your parents." Smiling, Jack looked down into brown eyes bright with indignation. How many times he'd seen that look, as if she could stand up to a grizzly and not flinch.

He'd missed this little spitfire more than he realized. And now she was back in his life . . . temporarily. Eventually she'd be far away in Hawaii if her crazy scheme worked. Maybe it wouldn't. Amy's plans had a way of falling through.

Watching her cheeks and the tip of her nose turn pink from the cold breeze at the front door, he had a very risky thought. He found himself wanting to kiss Amy Hobson.

ON SUNDAY AFTERNOON Amy walked into her parents' living room and faced a barrage of questions from her father. The hula contest and a photo of her had made the Sunday paper.

"Why didn't you tell us you were going to do this wild stunt?" From his leather recliner Virgil Hobson rustled a section of newspaper folded back to show a large black-and-white shot of Amy dancing. "I know you're always entering some tomfool contest, but parading around in forty-degree weather with no clothes on is ridiculous."

Amy's mother handed him a cup of coffee and walked over to sit beside Amy on the couch. "Maybe she had a reason for not telling us."

"Yeah, I'm sure she did. She knew I'd hit the ceiling. That was her reason."

Amy kept silent, forcing herself not to react to her father's bluster. Ever since his accident he'd compensated for his lack of mental quickness by an increased effort to intimidate anyone around him. His tactics hadn't worked with Amy because she was too much like him in spirit.

But her mother was another story. Consuela Hobson hadn't crossed her husband in anything since the day she'd become his seventeen-year-old bride in Manila. Almost twice her age and more than twice her size, the chief petty officer had dazzled her with his snappy uniform and tales of the wonderful life they'd have in the United States.

And their life had been wonderful, until the day came when Virgil was no longer capable of making all the decisions. Yet Amy knew her mother was still allowing him to make them.

"Well, Dad, would you feel better about the whole thing if Mom got a new gizmo for the kitchen out of the deal?"

"What gizmo?"

"A food processor. I have it out in the car."

"You do, do you?"

"It's pretty nifty, Dad. Slices, dices, peels, churns, blends, kneads and probably scratches your back if you push the right button."

Her mother murmured a protest. "I think you should keep your prize. After all, you won it."

"Me?" Amy laughed. "Come on, Mom."

"She's right, Connie." Her father smiled ruefully. "I'd hate to think what would happen if you turned Amy loose with such a machine."

"That's not the point, Dad. I could learn to use it. I just don't want to." Too late Amy realized she was reacting defensively, as she always did with her father.

"As I've said before, you can't expect to get a good man if you don't know your way around a kitchen."

She tried to temper her hostility. "Sure I can. I'll marry a good cook."

"Most men expect the woman to cook, too, Amy. As you know, one of the things that attracted me to your mother was her cooking. She still makes the best rice I've ever tasted, and I bet you're still using that microwave stuff."

"Yes, Dad. I'm hopeless." Amy gritted her teeth. Her father held such male-chauvinistic opinions that she'd probably never please him. "Do you want the food processor, Mom?"

"If you're sure you won't use it, Amy."

"Not a chance. I'll get it."

Her mother stood up. "Let me come with you. There's something . . ." Her voice trailed off and she glanced at her husband, who had already become absorbed in the sports page of the paper.

"Sure, Mom." She put an arm around her mother's shoulders and gave her a brief hug as they left the room. For the past few years Amy had felt more like a big sister than a daughter to this dainty, reserved woman who only came up to her chin. Amy sometimes wondered if strangers would believe they were related; the only characteristic they shared was the dark coloring of their eyes and hair.

"Don't let your father upset you, Amy," her mother said as they unhooked their coats from the hangers in the hall closet. "He really does care about you."

"I know." Amy put on her coat and opened the front door for her mother. "He cares for all of us, but he also thinks he knows what's right for everyone, and he doesn't."

Amy's mother said nothing.

"Mom," Amy persisted, knowing her comments were futile, "you can't let him rule the roost the way you do. He's not really capable of—"

"He's fine," her mother said abruptly. "Your father is fine."

Amy looked down at her mother's exotic features. She was always amazed that someone so delicate could also be so stubborn. Her mother's eyes, with their faint tilt, became expressionless at moments like this, and the flawless skin of her cheeks suggested a mask. Further discussion was useless and Amy knew it. "Okay, he's fine." She opened her car door and lifted the box from the front seat. "I think you'll love this food processor."

"I've always wanted one. But are you sure—"

"Yes, Mom. Would you please close the car door for me?"

"Amy, just a minute. Before we go back, I wanted to tell you something."

Amy turned with the large box in her arms. "What's that?"

"I know why you tried to win the trip to Hawaii."

3

AMY ALMOST DROPPED THE BOX. "You do?"

"Of course I do. You know how much your father wants to go to Hawaii. You haven't fooled me, Amy. That trip was supposed to be for us, wasn't it?"

"I—I—"

"Don't worry. I won't tell him and spoil your surprise. I think you're very smart, entering all these contests the way you do. They confuse me, but you seem to know all the tricks to win."

"Mom, it's not exactly what you—"

"Never mind. Let's go in and get out of the cold. I just wanted you to know that I understand what you're doing."

Amy couldn't think of a way to explain without spilling her entire plan. But now her mother thought that the trip, when Amy won it, would go to her parents. What a mess.

"By the way," her mother continued as they reentered the house, "how's Jack Blickensderfer? Wasn't he in that picture in the paper?"

"He's fine. In fact, I've offered to help him with his project of getting teenagers to read better. I'm going to tutor someone."

"You have? Why, that's wonderful, Amy. Why don't you tell your father about that?"

Amy put the box on the floor of the hall and took off her coat. "I think I'd rather not."

"Why?"

"He'd probably say I should spend my time going back to school myself, instead of teaching someone else."

"Well, he was disappointed that you didn't make good enough grades to get a scholarship, like Brad. But you still could take a few classes, maybe at night."

"In what, Mom? We've been over this a million times. I don't have the foggiest idea what I'd major in, so why waste the money? Brad always knew he wanted to be an engineer, but I've never had a drive like that."

Her mother closed the door of the coat closet. "I still think you should tell your father about tutoring those teenagers. And helping Jack. He always liked Jack."

Amy smiled. "So did I."

ALTHOUGH AMY DIDN'T TELL her father about the tutoring, she thought about very little else for the next few days. What had started out as a way to maintain a connection with Jack had become a personal challenge, a spark in a life that had become too humdrum lately.

Amy remembered her own struggles with English classes. She'd been able to read, but certainly hadn't enjoyed it much when it involved endless analyzing and book reports. She'd turned to novels of her own choosing, which she secreted inside the assigned textbook during the days she was supposed to be reading in class.

The novels were contemporary and fast-paced, but the student she would tutor, if Jack found her someone, might not have the skills to handle those novels.

Amy searched the bookstores and magazine counters for potential materials. She bought some rock magazines but no books. She had to wait and see who Jack found before she made any major purchases.

On Wednesday he called from the station. "Amy, I've only got two minutes while the record's on, but I've found someone for you. He's sixteen and his name's Steve. I'm off tomorrow night. Can you come to my apartment and meet him?"

"Sure can."

"I'm not far from you. I think my complex is owned by the same outfit as yours. Mine's called Mountainview."

Amy laughed. "And do you have one?"

"A mountain view? Doesn't everyone in Bellingham? They were safe with that name. It's a big mountain. Anyway, the number's 24B."

"Got it."

"Okay. See you tomorrow night. How's seven?" Without waiting for her answer, he hung up.

"Fine," Amy said into the dead telephone. "Nice talking to you, Jack. Glad you could call and chat."

His voice floated into the room from the radios. *"Here's an oldie but goodie for a special lady out there in Playland. Dust off the memories, those of you mature enough to remember this classic."*

When the soft sounds of Simon and Garfunkel's "Bridge Over Troubled Water" poured from the bank of small radios, Amy knew Jack had played the record for her. It was an old song; she must have been eight or nine when she'd first heard it.

Jack and Brad had been teenagers, barely, and Jack had brought the record over for Brad to hear. Amy had listened outside Brad's bedroom door and promptly decided the song was her all-time favorite. Whenever the boys had played records, she begged them to put on that particular one over and over.

In later years, when Amy had hit the swirling rapids of her own teenage years, she borrowed the record permanently and played it whenever times were tough. The song never failed to comfort her. It reminded her of Jack, the person who always seemed willing to be her own personal bridge over troubled waters. Then, somewhere in the process of moving out of her parents' house, she'd misplaced the record. How long had it been since she heard that song? Too long.

Good old Jack, she thought with a rush of warm feeling for him. Now she could do something to help his cause, for a change. She and Steve would get along fine. With her expert tutoring, Steve would be ready for literary classics after only a few weeks, and Jack would be so proud of her.

Amy went to sleep that night dreaming of the transformation she would make in her student, who would one day become a successful businessman or politician. Perhaps he'd be a doctor or scientist and find the cure for some dreaded disease. Then he would write a book in which he credited her, Amy Lorraine Hobson, as the one who had turned his life around.

The next evening she decided her dreams might have been a bit exaggerated, judging by the young man sitting across the room from her.

Steve Garrigan seemed destined for something less than world fame in his ragged Twisted Sister T-shirt and baggy cotton pants the color of used dishwater. The pants looked as if they might have come from the county garbage dump very recently. His only other protection against the cold November wind was a dirty flannel shirt that might once have been blue plaid.

One lock of his obviously permed hair was purple. The rest was pretty much the same shade of muddy brown and cut in various haphazard lengths of frizz that tended to fall over both eyes. Amy didn't doubt that he couldn't read. He probably couldn't see, either. Maybe that explained why his unlaced shoes didn't match.

Steve hadn't said much in the few minutes since he'd landed with a solid thump in the middle of Jack's sofa. Amy and Jack had each taken a chair, and Jack was trying to establish communication.

"So you like Twisted Sister?" Jack nodded toward the torn T-shirt.

Steve's response was unenthusiastic. "Yeah."

"Who else?"

"Most of them, I guess."

Jack nodded again and glanced at Amy.

She decided to try her hand. "Are you into any sports, Steve?"

"No."

"I bet you enjoy working on cars, though." Amy congratulated herself on that one. How else did his clothes get so dirty?

"I totaled my car last week."

"Oh, dear."

Steve shrugged. "It was a junk heap, anyway. But I couldn't get to work, so I got canned."

Amy looked over at Jack in dismay. This kid had nowhere to go but up. "Maybe a better job will come along," she said with determined cheer.

Steve's answer was another shrug. "So are you a teacher?"

"No, not exactly," Amy answered. She had to assume Steve was addressing her, although it was difficult to tell with his curtain of hair covering both eyes.

His tone was accusing. "Beeper said you were."

"Well, I offered to help with your English, so I guess in a way I'm a teacher."

"My reading," Steve corrected. "I don't read so great."

The admission was so honestly made that Amy's heart ached for him. Was there anything for this boy to be happy about? Nothing in his life seemed positive. Sure, she'd had a rough time in her teens, but nothing like this. Did Steve ever laugh, or even smile?

"You would like some help, then?" Amy asked, leaning toward him.

"Nothing much else to do. Might as well."

Amy pulled a folded paper out of her purse. "I remembered something from my high school days, something that worked really well for me." She stood up and walked over to Steve.

He shrank against the sofa. "You gonna make me read something out loud?"

"No." She handed him the paper. "This is a contract. I typed it up at work today."

Steve took the paper gingerly and scanned the single paragraph. "I don't know all these words."

"That's okay. This time you can trust me to tell you what's in this contract. Someday you might not be able to trust someone who asks you to sign something. That's one good reason to learn to read better."

"Beeper has contracts, but somebody else makes them up for him."

Amy glanced at Jack. This Beeper person was something. "And I'm sure Beeper trusts the person who writes up his contracts, but what if he had to rely on someone else one day, someone he didn't know?"

"That's what he says, too." Steve looked at the paper again. "Yeah, I guess contracts are important. So what does this one say?"

"That you and I will meet for an hour once a week for the next month, and that you'll spend at least two hours a week on the homework I give you."

"That's all?"

"That's all."

"Well, I can see how you'd know if I didn't do the first part, but how will you know if I put in two hours on the stuff you give me?"

"I won't know. Not really. But if you've signed a contract, you've made an honorable agreement, and I expect you to stand by it. Here's a pen."

"I put my name on this line at the bottom?"

"That's right. Below mine. I've already signed it."

Steve looked up. "So this is for you, too?"

"Yes. We're both agreeing to the terms. A high school teacher had me sign a contract once, and I took the work much more seriously after that, knowing that I'd put my name on the line."

Steve spread the paper on his knee and stared at it. "That makes sense, I guess," he said, and scrawled his name below Amy's. "Here you go." He handed the paper and pen back to her.

"Which night will be best for you?"

"Doesn't matter. Well, maybe not Friday or Saturday."

Amy smiled, hoping Steve had a girlfriend. At least that would be one bright spot in his otherwise gloomy life. "You'll be dating on the weekend?"

"Don't I wish. But who knows? Maybe I'll get lucky."

Amy didn't think Steve had even a nodding acquaintance with luck. "Then let's say Wednesday nights at seven, at my place. Are you close to the Bayview Apartments?"

"I can walk it."

"Number 106." Amy stood up and held out her hand. "Nice meeting you, Steve."

Steve scrambled to his feet and lightly took her hand. "Same here."

His hands were rough, and Amy guessed that his previous job had been dishwashing. Even in his loose handshake Amy could feel him trembling anxiously. Poor kid. Behind the scruffy clothes and the outrageous hair was a scared little boy. She wondered how he'd got up the nerve to come tonight.

Steve extracted his hand awkwardly and backed toward the door. "I'd better be going."

Jack walked with him to the door and touched him on the shoulder. "Congratulations for making it over here, Steve. That took some guts."

"Yeah." After another brief hesitation, Steve bolted out the door.

Amy slumped onto the sofa. "Oh, Jack, that poor boy. And there are lots of kids like him, you say?"

"Sure. They were there when we went to school, too. You said you dated them."

"No, I was wrong. I dated some wild boys, but they played a sport, or had a snazzy car, or something to hang on to. What has this poor fellow got?"

"Not much." Jack paced in front of her. "But now he's got you. I'm really grateful you suggested this, Amy. You've given me a whole new idea to go along with the reading club. I could organize a network of volunteers like you before we even get the building up."

"Sure you could. That's a terrific idea, Jack."

"It's really your idea." His blue eyes shone. "But I'm going to take it slow. The wrong volunteers could make a mess of things. You're kind and sensitive, but everyone might not relate well to a kid like Steve."

"I was worried when I first saw him. But he's hiding behind those clothes and that hair. When I figured that out, I didn't mind his looks anymore."

Jack sat down and took her by the shoulders. "And the contract was a real brainstorm. You're great, you know that?"

"Thanks." Her answering smile wobbled a little. His grip on her shoulders made her tingle in a way she'd never associated with Jack before. They used to touch all the time. Hugging was big in the Hobson family, and Jack was considered part of the family.

But the family was spread out now, with Brad and his wife in Spokane, and Amy across town in her own apartment. Amy decided she was just out of practice with this family touching stuff.

"Well, as Steve said, I guess I'd better be going," Amy remarked with a little laugh. "You must have things to do."

Jack removed his hands from her shoulders. "Beeper's coming over at eight."

"You spend your night off from the station tutoring a kid in reading?" Amy shook her head. "What would your fans think, Jack Bond?"

"They don't know. They assume I'm out with some gorgeous chick."

"Surely you do date."

"Yeah. I do have another night off—Sunday."

Amy wanted very much to ask if he had a steady relationship, but she didn't know how to state the question or exactly why she needed the answer. "I figured the Jack I knew couldn't have changed that much."

"Or the Amy I knew. Don't tell me you don't have a few guys following you around."

"A few," she said airily.

"But you're not really involved."

Amy shook her head. Well, Jack had no compunction about asking, but he'd always taken a proprietary interest in her. "I've been wary since Philip, I must admit. Besides, it wouldn't make sense for me to tie myself down right now, when I might be moving to Hawaii with my folks."

"I suppose not. Entered any new contests lately?"

"Three more this week. You didn't expect me to cry in my beer forever, did you?"

"I didn't notice you crying in your beer, period. You'll win your trip, Amy. Keep trying."

"And when I win, you'll be the first to know." She picked up her quilted ski jacket and put it on. "And then I can give away this jacket and my scarves and hats and gloves and boots and—"

"Sounds as if you're looking forward to the tropics."

"I am. I've never been much for this chilly damp weather. Cold robs me of spontaneity."

"What do you want to do, run around on the beach naked?" The minute the words were out, he wished he hadn't said them. All at once he got a very clear image of her doing just that.

She gave him a gamine smile, apparently unaware of his licentious thoughts. "Maybe."

He decided to change the subject, and fast. "Thanks again for taking Steve on. Call me if you want to talk about teaching methods."

"I have some ideas, but I probably will call before Wednesday, after I've thought more about how to start."

"Or come down to the station. You might enjoy it."

"Beard the lion in his den? Sure, why not? Well, see you later."

"So long, Amy."

Jack closed the door after her and stood there, hands shoved into his pockets, thinking. He'd better decide on a conscious plan of action or his natural response to Amy was going to take over.

The brown eyes that had once been innocent and mischievous now threatened to transform him into a raging creature of lust. He'd touched her tonight because he couldn't help himself.

She'd looked a little frightened, and that had been enough to keep him from taking her into his arms. What would she do if he did? She still seemed to think of him as a second big brother. If he reached for her as a man reaches for a desirable woman, she might recoil in horror. That would hurt. Besides, it would ruin the easy friendship they now enjoyed.

Still, he might take the chance, considering the possible rewards, except for one thing. Amy was shooting for Hawaii. What if her plans succeeded?

She wouldn't want to become entangled with a man between now and then, either. Not that she viewed him as a potential entanglement. She felt safe with him, and he'd be wise not to change that.

Maybe his attraction to her was just a phase, anyway. He hadn't seen her in a long time, and that first exposure—more like overexposure—had fired his imagination about the woman Amy had become. Probably after he'd been around her some more, gotten to know her again, she'd return to her original place in his thoughts—the place of the little sister.

The doorbell interrupted his reverie, and he was still close enough to the door to reach out and open it without moving.

"Wow, that was creepy! I didn't even hear your footsteps, man, before the door opened."

"Hi, Beeper."

The boy peered at Jack. "You okay? You look a little spaced. Say, a real hot chick passed me on the walkway. Do you know her? I thought to myself, that might be old Steve's teacher."

"It is."

"Uh-huh. Steve's a lucky guy."

"Want to switch with him?"

Beeper considered for a moment before shaking his head. "Nah. You're the man I need. Did you get the lyrics to the new Madonna number?"

"Right here." Jack crossed to a desk and took out some sheet music. "Let's see how well you can read the whole thing before we play the record."

"You're on." Beeper sprawled on the couch with the sheet music. As he studied the first page, a staccato noise sounded from the electronic instrument hooked to his belt. "Just a second, Jack. Can I use your phone?"

Jack nodded, hiding his smile. This happened at least twice every Thursday night. Beeper had quite an organization going.

The boy picked up the telephone on Jack's desk and dialed. "Beeper here. Whatcha need?"

Jack listened as Beeper gave detailed instructions on finishing a geometry assignment. Unlike Steve, Beeper was impeccably dressed in name-brand slacks and shirt. His clothes were clean, with just the right amount of wrinkle and slouch to be fashionable.

Every time Jack looked at Beeper, with his self-assured style and expensive clothes, he had to remind himself that the seventeen-year-old was reading on a fourth-grade level. And that represented progress over where he'd been when Jack had first started tutoring him.

Beeper hung up the phone and returned to the couch. "They always need so much direction," he said with a sigh.

"Wouldn't it be easier to do your own work?"

"And what would they do for extra money? I'm supporting half the school," Beeper argued.

"What happens when you graduate?"

"No problem. I'm training Steve to take my place."

DURING THE NEXT FEW WEEKS Jack kept waiting for the transformation, for Amy to once again become a familiar little sister, a sexless friend. It wasn't happening.

She was a regular visitor at the station, and each time she appeared he was more delighted to see her than the last time she arrived. Christmas came and went, and Amy signed Steve Garrigan to a new monthlong contract. Jack found two more volunteers, and his reading program began to take shape.

Amy and Jack compared notes and watched with pride as both Steve and Beeper developed their reading skills. Beeper began doing some of his own homework, but he found other jobs for his employees to keep them in spending money.

Through all the increased time spent with Amy, Jack had to exercise great restraint and remember to keep his hands to himself. He referred to Amy in front of his coworkers as "my adopted little sis." He hoped if he said it often enough, he would begin to believe that she was off limits. Instead she became more desirable than ever.

When she rushed in one night, fifteen minutes before he went off the air, Jack swore to himself as he watched her through the thick glass of the control booth. Damn, but she was delicious, with her cheeks glowing from the cold and excitement. How could he not kiss those laughing lips? He was alone at the station. To hell with propriety and her supposed plans. It was time she knew how he felt.

He switched on a commercial and cued the next record before motioning her into the booth.

"Can I talk?" Her voice was an excited whisper.

"Yep." He took off the headset and leaned back in his swivel chair while his gaze roamed in frustration over her bundled-up body. She was right. Washington *was* too cold for spontaneity.

"The most wonderful thing has happened." Her brown eyes glowed with happiness.

"Steve finished reading an entire issue of his hot-rod magazine."

"Better."

"He got a new car and a job."

"Better."

"Brad and Melissa are moving back to Bellingham."

"Better."

He closed his eyes. He'd known when she came in, but he hadn't wanted to admit it. Was that why he'd made the almost desperate decision to tell her his true feelings? Had he sensed he was close to losing her? "Let me cue this record and the commercial," he said, stalling.

She fidgeted impatiently while he worked.

"Okay. Back to the guessing game," he said at last.

"Come on, Jack. What have I been working for all this time?"

He should have been an actor, he thought as he feigned dawning recognition and happy surprise. "You won your trip, didn't you?"

"Yes!"

"Amy, that's great. You must be so excited." He could see she was. She didn't care that she might be on her way out of his life. Her dream for her parents and herself was coming true. "Was it one of the contest entries I gave you?" He hoped not.

"No, but I appreciate everything you've done. This time the contest was so easy! After all the jingles I've written, and that crazy hula I danced for your contest, I won by simply matching numbers on a national sweepstakes thing. Hawaii wasn't even the grand prize.

The grand prize was a house, if you can imagine. But I won the trip! Four days and three nights."

"Fantastic. That should be enough time to check out that property. When are you going?"

"As soon as possible. That's why I'm here."

"I can take Steve the same night I teach Beeper, if that's your problem."

"No. I'll work that out with him. We're about to negotiate a new contract, anyway. I'm here because I have a proposition for you."

"Oh?"

"The trip is for two, Jack. I want you to come with me."

4

"RUN THAT BY ME once more?" Jack was sure he'd misunderstood. Amy couldn't be asking him to go along with her to Hawaii, unless . . . Was it possible that she was interested in him, had been battling some of the same emotions he had?

"It's the only way I can keep my parents from becoming suspicious about the trip."

"Oh." So much for her intentions toward him. "But why not one of your girlfriends?"

"None of them knows anything about Hawaii, and you do. The trip only takes me to Oahu, and my property's on Maui. I'm sure you know all about the interisland flights and how to get around. Please, Jack. You'd help me a lot."

He decided to buy some time to think. Going to Hawaii with her was either a very good idea or a very bad one, and he couldn't figure out which. "We've got the news coming up in two minutes and then I'm finished for the night. How about if we go somewhere and talk about this?"

"That's fine."

A little puzzled by Jack's reluctance, Amy left the control booth and strolled out to the lobby. She'd thought a trip to Hawaii would be fun for Jack, a chance to visit some old haunts. Yet he hadn't been particularly enthusiastic. She plopped on a couch and leafed through an old issue of *Time*.

"All set," he announced, pulling on his coat as he entered the lobby. "How about pie and coffee?"

"Sounds good. We can take my car and then I'll bring you back. It's raining, by the way."

"So said our weatherman."

"I keep forgetting that you're a deejay. You know everything, I guess." Amy ducked out the door and hurried to unlock her Volkswagen Rabbit. She leaned over quickly to unlatch Jack's door, but by the time he got in, his hair was already sprinkled with rain. The drops sparkled for a moment when the interior light of the car flashed on.

No doubt about it, Amy decided; Jack was nice to look at. Maybe he had better things to do than take a trip with his old buddy's little sister, even if Hawaii was the destination. Amy pressed her lips together and started the car. She didn't relish being rejected.

"No, I don't, by the way," he said, rubbing his hands together and blowing on them.

"Don't what?"

"Know everything."

"You and Brad used to act as if you did."

"Most guys do at eighteen. But seriously, please don't think I can make this Hawaii thing turn out for you just because I've been there."

"You don't want to go, do you?"

"I didn't say that."

"Look, Jack, don't spare my feelings. If the idea of taking a trip with Brad's baby sister rates up there with having a root canal on a back molar, forget it."

"Amy, that's not the problem."

"Have you got a girlfriend I don't know about who would be insanely jealous?"

"No, I don't."

Amy laughed with relief. "Then why the stalling tactics? I thought you'd enjoy a free trip."

"Let's back up a little. I'm not really clear about why anyone has to go with you in the first place, and why you couldn't ask another woman in the second place."

Amy hesitated, and the silence was broken only by the wiper blades squeaking across the windshield.

"You've got something up your sleeve, Amy. Spill it."

"Uh . . . my mother got it into her head that I was trying to win a trip so I could give it to her and Dad as a present. I didn't have the heart to tell her otherwise. So when I break the news that I'm using the trip myself, it'll look more logical if I have a traveling companion already—a man. She'll be thrilled if I'm taking you."

Now it was Jack's turn for several seconds of thoughtful silence. "Amy Lorraine Hobson, are you planning to mislead your mother into thinking we're romantically involved?"

Amy cleared her throat. "Well . . . sort of, but for a good cause, Jack. How can I explain that I'm going to Hawaii because I've bought some land for them and I have to check on it? Please, you have to go with me, or my whole scheme will be in jeopardy."

"That's quite a responsibility you're shouldering me with."

"I know, but you're the only man I can trust to take with me."

"Maybe I should send Cousin Ernie," Jack muttered, leaning his head back against the car seat. He didn't like the way this was going. The only one she could trust? Where did that leave him? Probably in Frustration City. "I wonder if you've thought this through," he said, raising his head at last.

"Of course I have! Doggone it, nobody gives me credit for having any sense around here. Will I ever live down my reputation as Brad's featherbrained sister?"

"Hey, that isn't quite what I meant."

"What did you mean?"

"I meant that your trip for two will only give you one room and maybe only one bed."

"Jack, luxury hotel rooms usually have two beds in them these days. Look, if you don't want to go, say so. I really don't have to know the reason."

"It's not that I don't want to go. I just thought you might feel uncomfortable sharing a room with me, that's all."

"That's silly, Jack. We're almost like brother and sister, aren't we? After all the times you stayed overnight at our house, this will be nothing." She glanced at him. "Could it be that you'll feel uncomfortable sharing a room with me? I promise not to hog the bathroom or leave my nylons hanging over the shower rod."

Jack closed his eyes briefly. Was she really so unaware of the effect she had on him? "I wasn't worried about that, either."

"Then why not say yes?" She swung into the parking lot of an all-night coffee shop.

He felt the decision coming, and he was afraid it was the wrong one for both of them. Amy hadn't a clue about what would happen on this trip, but he had a pretty good idea. Unless she refused to have anything to do with him, they wouldn't spend their nights in separate beds. And then what? She still planned to move to Hawaii eventually.

"Jack, you're driving me crazy. Yes or no?"

"I'd have to arrange for vacation days at the station." This was it. He'd surrendered to the incredible temptation of spending three nights alone in a hotel with Amy Hobson.

"That seems easy enough." She switched off the ignition.

"When do you want to go?" He heard the tremor in his voice and hoped she hadn't.

"As soon as possible, but I have to check with the lumberyard to see when I can get off. How about, say, in three weeks?"

In the dim light shining from the coffee shop windows he searched her face for any indication that she was feeling the same uncertainty and excitement he felt. Instead, her expression was matter-of-fact, as if he really were a big brother, an asexual friend. Unless her attitude changed, he wouldn't have the courage to take their relationship further. But after all, weren't they going to Hawaii, a place famous for romance and passion?

"Can you make it in three weeks, Jack?" Amy prompted.

"Sure," he said with a smile. "Why not?"

WITH SOME FAST TALKING Amy persuaded Jack to go with her to her parents' house on Sunday and break the news of the trip they would be taking together. They drove over in Jack's Camaro and pulled into the driveway behind Virgil Hobson's old pickup. The battered hood was up, and Amy's father was bent over the carburetor with an oily rag in one hand. At the sound of the car in the driveway, he straightened up. His eyes widened as Jack and Amy got out of the shiny black vehicle.

"Jack Blickensderfer!" he said, wiping his hands on the rag and striding forward. "Does that machine belong to you?"

"Yes, sir. Or it will in a few years." He shook Virgil's outstretched hand.

"You always did love fancy cars. You and Brad. He's got a Corvette now."

"I think he sold that, Dad," Amy reminded him gently. "Remember, when Penny was born they decided on a bigger car?"

"Did they?" Her father looked puzzled. "I can't keep track of all these changes everybody's making. That's why I hang on to old Bessie here." He patted the truck's back fender and left his large handprint in the dust. "Everything's still simple under the hood. I'll bet it takes a mechanical engineer to work on that thing of yours, Jack."

"Yeah, I admit that's a disadvantage." Jack glanced over his shoulder at the car. "But it's fun to drive. Want to take it for a spin?"

Amy's father shook his head. "Not me. Is that why you two are over here? To give an old man a ride in a sports car?"

"No, Dad." Amy smiled at him. "I have some exciting news. I finally won a trip to Hawaii, and I've asked Jack to go with me."

"No kidding? You mean all that contest business finally came to something? I always figured you were wasting your time when you could have been doing something more constructive, like going to school."

Amy stuck her hands in her coat pockets. "Well, I won a trip. I guess that's worth something."

"Yeah, it's nice. Of course it won't get you a better job or anything, but it's nice." Her father paused to glance at Jack. "And you're taking this guy with you? I didn't know you two were even dating."

Amy squared her shoulders. "We've been seeing each other pretty regularly, and Jack's the perfect person to take along, because he's been there. He can show me around."

"I suppose so." Her father wiped his hands with the rag again, although they didn't need it. "You're a grown woman now, Amy. I suppose you can do what you want, with whoever you want."

"Mr. Hobson, Amy and I aren't—" Jack began and then stopped himself. He and Amy weren't what? And whatever their status now, he expected it to change before they came back from Hawaii. So what was he planning to assure her father about? This whole business was very awkward, and his sensible side wished he'd never agreed to the trip. His emotional side, on the other hand, wished he and Amy were already on the plane.

Amy gave an exaggerated shiver. "It's getting cold out here, Dad. I'm going inside to tell Mom. Coming, Jack?"

"Sure." He didn't want to go through this again with her mother, but he didn't relish staying outside and facing more questions from her father, either. "See you later, Mr. Hobson."

"Right."

As they walked toward the front door, Amy spoke in a low tone. "Just let them think whatever they want to about us, Jack, okay?"

"I feel damned strange about this, Amy," he mumbled in reply. "I never thought I'd be announcing to your father that I was about to sleep with his daughter. He's not crazy about the idea, you know."

"We can explain everything to him later, after I'm sure the land is what they want. And he's right. I'm a grown woman now, way beyond his jurisdiction."

"Are you?"

Amy paused with her hand on the front doorknob. "What's that supposed to mean?"

"You're going through an awful lot of trouble to please him, Amy."

She frowned. "I'm only restoring what is rightfully his, Jack. His and Mom's. I explained all that."

"And I still think you shouldn't take on the task alone, as if the problem were yours to solve. They're grown-ups, too, aren't they?"

"In some ways, yes. In other ways, no. I have to do this, Jack. Will you help me or not?"

He sighed. "I'll help you."

"Then let's go in. Mom will love seeing you again." Amy opened the door and called to her mother.

The tiny woman ran forward when she saw Jack and stood on tiptoe to hug him. "Jack! What a wonderful surprise!"

Jack returned her embrace with a boyish smile that tugged at Amy's heart. As Amy took off her coat she thought about what he'd said that night over pizza concerning his own parents and his lack of any real relationship with them.

"It's great to see you again, Mrs. Hobson," Jack said, holding her at arm's length. "You look terrific."

"I'm getting old," Amy's mother protested with a wave of her hand.

"Never." Jack grinned at her. "You always were the best-looking one of the family."

"How can you say that, Jack?" Amy's mother walked over and put an arm around her daughter's waist. "Especially with our little Amy growing into such a beauty."

"Mother, really." Amy's face grew hot.

"And don't think I haven't noticed." Jack shrugged out of his coat. "But I'll bet she can't cook like you can, Mrs. Hobson."

Awareness teased Amy's nerves at Jack's casual comment on her looks. Was he playing a role for her mother's benefit, or did he really consider her attractive? Amy wished she knew which.

"Cooking's not everything," Amy's mother said. "This girl is very clever and I bet someday she'll surprise us all with what she can do."

"Well, I've already done something, Mom." Amy put both hands on her mother's small shoulders and took a deep breath before speaking her next words in a rush. "I've won a Hawaiian trip for two and Jack and I are going together. Isn't that wonderful?"

"A . . . a trip to Hawaii?"

Amy nodded.

"But I thought . . . Well, of course that's wonderful!" Amy's mother smiled brightly. "I had no idea that you two were, uh, that you and Jack—"

"Just recently, Mom. This trip will give us a chance to get away together for a little while." As Amy spoke the words, she felt a tremor pass over her again. She glanced at Jack with a new awareness of how he might seem to someone who hadn't known him forever. And he would seem like a very desirable man.

"Well, that's . . . nice. Did you tell Dad?"

"Yes, they told me." Her father had come through the front door unnoticed. "What do you think, Connie?"

"I think they make a nice couple, Virgil."

"Hmph. I'd say they're taking the honeymoon a little early. Putting the cart before the horse."

"That's how young people do things these days, Virgil."

Amy looked sideways at Jack and noticed the nervous way he was shifting his weight from one foot to the other. He obviously hated risking the disapproval of these two people who had been so kind to him. Amy regretted his discomfort, but how else could she carry out her plan?

"I suppose," her father said gruffly. "Anyway, I came to see if anyone was fixing lunch in here."

"I'll get right to it," Amy's mother said quickly. "And you two will stay, won't you?"

Amy's father clapped Jack on the shoulder. "Might as well. Great game coming up in a few minutes on TV. Celtics and the Lakers."

Jack looked surprised. "Didn't they play last Sunday?"

"Did they? I thought they were this Sunday. Well, somebody's playing something this afternoon. Come on in and see the new set Brad gave us for Christmas this year. Biggest damned screen I ever saw."

Amy watched them go into the living room and shook her head. "Brad gave you that set two years ago, Mom."

"It doesn't matter, does it? Come on in and help me with lunch."

"When you got the set doesn't matter," Amy agreed, following her mother into the kitchen. "But Dad's losing track of all kinds of details. Before I leave I'd better go over the checkbook and make sure he's up-to-date on the bills."

Amy's mother opened the refrigerator door and began pulling out containers of food and putting them on the counter with unnecessary force. "You know I don't approve of you snooping into his papers, Amy."

"Mom, they're your papers, too, even though you refuse to have anything to do with them. And Dad's not the manager he used to be. He forgets things."

"Not often."

"Often enough. What about the time the gas was turned off because the check didn't arrive on time for the second month in a row?"

"I wish I hadn't called you about that." Amy's mother organized pots and pans on the stove, still not looking at her daughter. "I tried to reach your father, but he was test-driving that big Cadillac he works on so often, and Jerry didn't know when he'd be back. I had to cook dinner, and I didn't know what to do."

"What you do, Mom, is take over paying the bills. Then things like that won't happen."

Finally her mother turned to Amy with a stricken expression. "Your father would have a fit if I even suggested such a thing. He's always been in charge of all our finances. You know that."

"Yes, and it's a big mistake, Mom. You need to take more responsibility, start handling a few things—"

"That's unnecessary, Amy." Her mother turned her back and opened a utensil drawer. "Your father is fine. He's taken care of me very well for thirty years, and I'm not about to doubt him now."

"Mom, will you please listen for once?"

Her mother turned from the stove and brandished the spoon she was holding. "No, Amy, you listen to me. Virgil Hobson is a fine man, and the navy was wrong to put him on disability after the accident. He still should be doing his old job with the motor pool, instead of working at some little garage repairing other people's cars. I'm not going to make him even more miserable by taking over his job at home, too. Besides, you know I don't understand all that paperwork."

Amy clenched her hands in frustration. Her mother wasn't going to admit how inept her father had become since the accident. Consuela Hobson was living in the same dream world she'd inhabited for thirty years, a world in which her husband would shelter her from all harm for the rest of her life.

"Mom, I'll be in Hawaii nearly five days, and I'm worried that something might happen while I'm gone. You won't have me to call, so I think we'd better find out if the bills have been paid and the banking done, because—"

"You don't have to worry about us." She lifted her round chin. "I can see that you have your own life to lead."

"Mom, I'm sorry that I couldn't give that trip to you and Dad."

Her mother's laugh sounded forced. "Forget I ever mentioned it. Going over there would only stir up buried dreams. We're better off staying here and forgetting about Hawaii."

"I guess." Amy turned away, afraid in another moment she'd reveal her entire plan to her mother, just to bring the light of hope to those dark eyes. But Amy knew enough not to say anything yet. The plan had to be complete, the deal perfect before she brought her parents into it. Otherwise, this whole idea could end up being discarded, labeled another one of little Amy's harebrained escapades and dismissed as foolish.

She could almost hear Brad's laughter if he found out what she was trying to do. Well, she'd show him. She'd show them all.

5

THREE WEEKS LATER when the plane landed at the Honolulu airport on Oahu, Amy reached for Jack's hand.

He decided the gesture was unconscious; she would have held almost anyone's hand in an effort to share her excitement. But he enjoyed the contact, anyway. "You did it, kid," he said gently.

"Yep." She gave him a quick smile before her attention went back to the small window beside her. "The sun is shining," she said with a touch of reverence.

"Of course. That's the law around here."

"Okay, maybe that was a dopey thing to say, but I'm so used to fog and mist and rain in Bellingham, especially in February. This is like another world, with the sun and the palm trees. Do they still meet everyone who gets off the plane and put leis around our necks?"

"I don't think so. The jumbo jets probably made that little custom obsolete."

"Oh. Well, it doesn't matter." Amy kept her nose pressed to the window as the plane rolled to a stop and the passengers began wrestling with their carry-on luggage.

Jack touched her shoulder. "Amy, we can get off now. If you'll turn loose of that window, you can see a whole lot more from outside the plane."

"What?" She turned a startled gaze toward him and then grinned sheepishly. "I can't help staring, Jack. Hawaii looks so warm."

"I guess it does." He took a moment to enjoy the anticipation glowing in her brown eyes. He wondered if that kind of eagerness would ever be connected with her feelings for him. Right now she didn't seem to have room to consider anything but this plan for her parents. "Let's go," he said, and unbuckled his seat belt.

Once inside the airport, they went to the terminal where interisland trips were booked. Jack arranged a flight for the next morning to take them to the neighboring island of Maui.

"I wish we could go now," Amy said, looking wistfully at a colored poster of the island where the land development was located.

"There's just not time, Amy. We could fly over and back before tonight, but that drive to Hana sounds murderous. We'd never make it to the airport for the last flight back to Oahu."

"You're right, but—"

"Hey, you're supposed to be on vacation, and the brochure says we get a free luau on the beach tonight. You wouldn't want to miss that, would you?"

Amy glanced up at him. What was the matter with her? She was in Hawaii with a very good-looking man, even if he was almost like a brother; the moon would be full tonight, and they had tickets to a luau. Her parents' land would still be there tomorrow, and the next day for that matter. There was no rush whatsoever. "No," Amy said, linking her arm through his, "I don't want to miss a thing."

"Good." Jack steered her toward a line of hotel courtesy vans parked near the curb. "You wait here and I'll get the luggage."

"Okay." After he walked away, Amy consulted her watch. Three o'clock. They had time for a swim on Waikiki Beach before the luau. Maybe she'd even try for a bit of a suntan or build a sand castle. Swimming in February! She smiled at the thought.

While she waited she became engrossed in watching the vacationers pile cheerfully into the courtesy vans. Not many families traveled to Hawaii at this time of year, Amy concluded. But there were couples of varying ages and several groups of older women. Amy noticed the independent way the older ladies conducted themselves and tried to imagine her mother in such a group. She couldn't. What kind of life would her mother have if she became a widow someday? Amy didn't like the answer to that question.

"What a long face for such a pretty wahine." Jack's rich voice boomed right beside her. When she glanced up, he held a necklace of lavender flowers aloft. "Aloha," he said, and draped the lei around her neck. "Welcome to Hawaii." Then in one smooth motion he kissed her on both cheeks.

"Jack!" Amy touched her warm cheeks and laughed with a mixture of delight and surprise. She could still feel the press of his lips against her skin, and her heart beat erratically. "How sweet of you." She held the baby orchids up to her nose. "Where did you get this?"

"Ye olde tourist stand inside." He thrust his hands in his pockets and looked pleased with himself. "I guess the locals can't afford to give them away anymore, but sentimental types can still buy them."

"And you are sentimental."

"Yeah."

"Thanks, Jack."

"My pleasure. I figured no lady should attend a luau without one. Come on, let's find our van."

The total impact of sharing a hotel room with Jack didn't hit Amy until they were standing outside the eighth-floor room and Jack turned the key in the lock of the door, their door, the one they would both be behind tonight. Amy tried convincing herself that Jack wasn't any different from Brad. Occupying the same room was no big deal.

Except that Brad had never given her a necklace of orchids. Well, hadn't she almost asked for them? Jack was only being nice to someone he considered a little sister.

Jack swung the door wide and motioned Amy inside. "Home sweet home for the next four days."

Amy walked past him with as much nonchalance as she could muster. There were two beds, as she had predicted, but the space between them was very small. She hurried over to the heavy drapes and pulled the cord to open them. "Do you suppose we can see the ocean from this balcony?"

"Lanai," Jack corrected, setting the two suitcases on the floor.

"What?" Amy unlocked the sliding glass door and pushed it back.

"In Hawaii they call balconies 'lanais.' Let's see what's out here."

They stepped onto the balcony together and each took a different end to lean over the railing.

"Just more buildings," Amy said with a sigh.

"Figures." Jack grinned at her. "After all, this isn't the Oceanview Hotel."

Amy made a face. "And I imagined sitting on the balcony, I mean the lanai, and watching the moon on the water."

"We'll have to stroll the beach if you want to do that." Jack braced his palms against the railing and looked down at the bustling Honolulu traffic.

"That's an idea." Amy glanced sideways at him. Stroll the beach in the moonlight with Jack? Why did that picture seem so exciting? It wasn't as if she thought of him in a romantic sense. And yet, she couldn't help noticing how the short sleeves of his knit shirt hugged his biceps. She'd never thought of Jack as having strong arms, but she was thinking it now.

He pushed away from the railing and faced her. "We might as well unpack. Which bed do you want?"

Amy glanced through the open glass door at the two beds with a mere two feet between them. "Doesn't matter." She stared at an office building across from their hotel rather than look at Jack. Sleeping in the same room with him was taking on a tinge of eroticism she hadn't anticipated. "You choose. I'm going to freshen up." She paused and felt her cheeks grow hot. "That is, unless you want to use the—"

"That's okay. You go ahead." His tone revealed his own uneasiness.

"Okay." Amy bolted through the open door, grabbed the small makeup case she'd carried on the plane and dashed into the bathroom. Why, oh, why, had she imagined this trip with Jack would be such a breeze?

Something was happening to the brother-sister relationship they'd once shared. When they were younger, they'd practically lived together at times. She could remember Jack or Brad banging on the upstairs bathroom door when they'd thought she was spending too much time on her makeup or her hair. But that sort of good-natured pestering had vanished from their relationship. And because of that, Amy felt suddenly shy about living with him in such close quarters.

And that moment, when she'd looked at him leaning on the railing... She'd never been aware of his body before. Sure, she knew lots of girls considered him handsome, and she did, too, in a way. But acknowledging that Jack was attractive was one thing. Gazing with lust at his muscles was something else. Amy wondered what sort of explosive situation she'd gotten herself into.

When she emerged from the bathroom she found Jack hanging his slacks and shirts in the closet, and she realized her clothes would be nestled right beside his, as if she and Jack were newlyweds. But they weren't. They were just friends, old friends. At least they used to be.

"Your turn," she said lightly. "What do you say—after we get settled shall we hit the beach?" The plan sounded better now than it had at the airport. Anything to leave the confines of this room, which was far too small, far too cozy.

"Great idea." Jack turned to his suitcase that lay open on the nearest bed and picked up another shirt. "As you see, I decided to take the bed next to the door."

"That's fine." She realized instinctively that the choice had been a protective one, a way to put himself between Amy and any potential intruders. Jack was taking care of her, but was he doing so out of chivalrous kindness, or something more?

He crossed to the dresser with a pile of underwear and Amy turned away. She didn't want to know anything about his underwear. Thinking about his underwear led to thinking about . . . oh, no. She didn't know what he slept in. Maybe nothing. She'd brought a no-nonsense pair of pajamas and a light bathrobe, but now that she thought of them, they might be a trifle thin. She'd just have to wear a bra and panties underneath.

But what about Jack? She should have discussed this with him before they left. Maybe he'd brought a bathrobe and he'd put it on as soon as he got out of bed. Amy laid her suitcase on the bed with a thump and zipped it open impatiently. She had to get off this kick, and fast. What difference did it make what Jack wore to bed? She could always look the other way if the sight of him disturbed her so much.

Jack closed his suitcase and set it on the closet floor. "I'll go change into a suit and we'll walk to the beach. I'm sure it's not far."

"Great. I'll change out here." Amy flashed him a smile. After he'd closed the bathroom door she dug through her suitcase for her bathing suit, stripped down in record time and wiggled into her Lycra one-piece. She'd considered a bikini for the trip and discarded the idea. After all, she was on this vacation with good old Jack, not someone she was trying to impress. She shoved her arms into a black mesh cover-up and pulled her sandals from a side pocket of the suitcase.

By the time Jack came out of the bathroom, she was hanging the rest of her clothes beside his in the closet.

She deliberately left a good foot of space on the rod between his hangers and hers.

"I'm ready if you are."

"Almost." Amy flicked a glance over her shoulder and swallowed a gulp of surprise. With another covert peek she watched him lay his clothes over a chair and toss his wallet on the desk. How could she not think of a body like that?

The white hotel towel he'd draped over his shoulders couldn't disguise the fact that Jack had filled out since high school. Dark, curling hair shadowed his chest, softening the imposing breadth of it and inviting the touch of her fingers. His skimpy navy-blue swim trunks emphasized the narrowness of his hips, but more than that, the stretch material outlined the part of Jack that Amy had been struggling to pretend didn't exist.

She'd never pictured Jack that way, never imagined what it would be like to— No, she wouldn't allow her imagination to continue on such a dangerous path. He'd probably laugh if he knew the crazy direction of her thoughts.

"That should take care of everything," she said, closing the louvered closet door. "Can we go like this?"

"You bet. We're in Honolulu. Besides, we're only about two blocks from the beach, by my calculations." He pushed his feet into rubber thongs lying beside his bed. "We'll leave a room key at the desk and I'll take some cash for the water cycles."

"The what?"

"You'll see." He walked to the desk and took some bills from his wallet. "I know you'll want to try them."

"But they cost money. If we're going to do anything that costs money, I should pay. You've already bought me the lei, and—"

"Amy, don't be silly. You've given me the whole trip, so the least I can do is treat you to a few of the little things Hawaii has to offer. And speaking of the lei, where is it?"

"Hanging over there on the headboard of my bed."

"Let's put it in a sinkful of water." He crossed to her bed. As he picked up the necklace one of the tiny flowers fell on the bedspread.

"Oh, no," Amy cried. "I hope it's not falling apart."

"Nope. Just this one came off." He brought the flower to her. "That's okay. You need something for your hair, anyway."

"I do?"

"Definitely. Required dress around here. Hold this." He handed her the lei and smoothed her hair back before tucking the blossom behind her ear. "Now you look like a true Hawaiian maiden."

Amy stood very still and breathed in the delicate fragrance of the tiny orchid mixed with the musky scent of Jack's after-shave. His fingers brushing the curve of her ear had infused her body with languid heat, and she looked lazily into his eyes, not wanting to break the delicious spell he had cast over her.

Jack gazed down at Amy, and his pulse began to race. There. That was the look he'd been waiting for. Soft yet aware. Aware of him. He could kiss her now, but he was afraid to push his luck. She might not be used to her feelings yet. His kiss might startle that dreamy expression right off her face. A kiss would change everything, wouldn't it?

But her lips were so close. He longed to trace the graceful sweep of her pink mouth with the tip of his finger. And then perhaps with the tip of his tongue, and then . . . And then he might not be able to stop easily. And he didn't think she was ready for what he had in mind. Not yet.

"Let's—" He stopped to clear his throat. "Let's check out the beach before the sun goes down." He chucked her under the chin. "We'll never get a tan standing around here, kid."

Amy swallowed and turned away. Kid. That was how he thought of her, no matter what expression she'd imagined in his eyes a moment earlier. Oh, he liked her well enough, probably even felt some affection for his best friend's little sister. But other than that, other than the ties of familiarity that had been formed over the years, he had no particular interest in her as a woman.

They walked the sunny sidewalks to the beach in silence. Amy tried to convince herself that she should be grateful Jack had agreed to accompany her on the trip in the first place. He would be a tremendous help the next day, when she had to find the land development on the far side of Maui. And he was nice to have around even at that moment. What fun would she have going to the beach alone?

Amy glanced around her and couldn't help being caught up in the gaiety. The scene was splashed with color, from the natural brilliance of pink and purple flowers to the flamboyant tropical designs worn by the people on the streets. She could figure out how long anyone had been in Hawaii by the darkness of each tan. She and Jack were very pale, compared with most of the brightly clad people they passed on the sidewalk.

"Here's where we take off our shoes," Jack said as they filed down a narrow public path to the beach.

"Oh, Jack, how beautiful." Amy slipped off her sandals and hurried forward over the warm sand. She wound her way through the maze of towels and sunbathers until she reached the cool dampness just above the waterline. Then she walked forward until the froth of the advancing waves tickled her toes. "Jack! The water is warm!"

Jack came to stand beside her. "A little different from Lake Whatcom, huh?"

"I've never felt such warm water. I'm going to love this, Jack."

"The beach isn't very secluded, I'm afraid."

"But so alive! Just look at the sailboats and yachts. And there goes a motorboat pulling someone up in a parasail!"

"Want to try it?"

Amy started to say yes but then realized such excitement could be expensive. "I'll stick to those," she said, pointing to what looked like oversize tricycles for two careering around, their huge colored tires balancing them on top of the water. "Isn't that what you were talking about? Come on, Jack, let's rent one!"

She sprinted across the sand and Jack followed at a more leisurely pace, the better to enjoy her enthusiasm. Maybe the exuberance of crowded Waikiki Beach was exactly what they needed right now, rather than some quiet stretch of sand where they'd have to confront their feelings for each other directly.

They were given a water cycle with bright blue wheels, and they began pedaling frantically and laughing as their unwieldy craft bounced along on the waves and occasionally collided with other cycles.

"Why don't they tip over?" Amy asked after a particularly jouncing wave doused them with warm salt water on impact.

"Good stability, I guess. They can ride out the turbulence underneath."

"Like a bridge over troubled water?"

He gazed into her warm brown eyes. "Yeah, kind of like that." He wanted so much to kiss her. So much. He looked away with an effort. "This trike is pretty nifty, wouldn't you say?"

Amy would have given anything to know what he'd been thinking just then. But the spell had been broken once more. "It would be even niftier if you'd pedal, Jack. I'm doing all the work here."

"Yes, but have you stopped pedaling long enough to look down? You can see the bottom, and I bet it's at least fifteen feet below us."

"Look at those beautiful fish!" Amy leaned over the cycle and almost lost her balance.

Jack grabbed her around the waist and hauled her back onto her seat. "Don't go falling overboard, Hobson. I'd have a devil of a time pulling you back up on this thing."

Amy clasped her hands together and batted her eyelashes at him. "My hero. You saved my life."

Jack grinned. "Darn right. Those fish down there could be man-eating barracuda, for all you know."

Amy clutched his arm. "Oh, Jack, do you think so? Let's go back to shore. Now."

"No, I don't really think so, but you sure are fun to tease, Amy."

"You should know. You've been doing it long enough."

"You lost your flower."

"Did I?" She reached for the place behind her ear where he'd tucked the small orchid. "There it is, floating on that wave. It must have dropped when I looked down at the fish."

"Let's get it back." Jack turned the cycle in the direction of the flower and started pedaling.

"Jack, you're crazy," Amy said with a laugh, but she began pedaling, too.

"Now you keep this thing going, and I'll lean over and pluck it from the water, just like the cowboys used to do with their hats."

"What if you fall in? What if those fish really are barracuda?"

"They're not, and I won't fall in. I'm your hero, remember? Heroes never make fools of themselves."

"True. But if you lose a grip on hero-hood, I haven't got the strength to help you back up here."

"You won't have to. Just pedal." Jack leaned far over the water as they approached the bobbing piece of lavender. "That's it. Steer a little to the right. Keep pedaling; keep pedaling . . . There! Got it."

He swung back into his seat and presented her with the dripping flower. "Your posy, madam."

She took the wet flower and placed it in her equally wet hair. "How's that?"

"Extremely fetching."

"You saved the day again. How can I ever thank you?"

"The time-honored way, of course."

Amy cocked her head at him, considering. Then she wound one moist arm around his neck, kissed him swiftly and platonically on the lips and released him. "Like that?"

Jack regarded her steadily. "Sort of."

"What do you mean, sort of?"

He let the cycle rise and fall of its own accord on the ocean swells as he rested one arm across the back of the seat and looked at her. "I mean true gratitude is more like this." He pulled her against his damp chest and brought his mouth down on hers.

6

THERE WAS NOTHING PLATONIC about his kiss. His lips when they met hers were open, his tongue seeking to explore the secret recesses of her mouth. Amy stiffened and pulled away.

Jack gazed at her steadily and then he sighed. "Your eyes are wide as saucers. Apparently I've shocked you, Amy."

She touched her trembling lips. "I—I didn't think that you—"

"Could react like any normal man with regard to you?"

"But we've always been like sister and brother."

"Is that how you want it to stay?"

"I don't know." She glanced shyly at him and then looked out at the ruler-straight line of the horizon. "When we were younger I got mad at you a lot, but having you around was always...reassuring. You were a friend, Jack. Maybe the best one I ever had as a kid growing up. I'd hate for that to change."

"Amy, you can't play the flip side of a record without turning it over."

She thought for a while as the cycle rocked lazily on the waves. "Maybe I don't want to hear the flip side."

"And maybe you do. You kissed me first."

"I know. That's why I'm so confused, Jack. Perhaps I was egging you on, trying to find out what would happen."

"And now that you found out, you're not happy with the situation?"

"I didn't say that. But all of a sudden I realized that if our relationship...changes, we can never go back to the way everything used to be."

"That's true. It's known as growing up."

Amy gazed silently into the clear water.

"I didn't think you knew quite what you were doing by asking me to go on this trip." He caressed her shoulder. "But you must have realized, even before we left, that we are different people from the two kids we used to be. You've become a beautiful woman, Amy."

She turned and studied his face.

"Very beautiful," he added softly.

"I thought maybe when you made that remark to my mother you were being nice."

Jack shook his head. "I could have been but I wasn't."

"Oh." She couldn't completely repress a smile of feminine satisfaction. "But you've never asked me out or anything."

"No, I haven't, partly because I've been reluctant to change an easy pattern, too, especially when I noticed how quickly you fell back into the old ways. But the main problem for me is your decision to move to Hawaii when your parents do. That's a long way from Bellingham. What sort of future would any relationship between us have?"

Amy considered the concept of a "relationship" with Jack. The thought gave her goose bumps, and that was bad. He was right. Even if they were willing to trade their old friendship for something more intimate, a romance between them made no sense. Yet she could see how they'd been moving toward this kiss ever since they met on the stage at the Cascade Mall.

"Jack, I've blundered into a mess and pulled you in with me. I'm sorry."

"You're not the only one at fault. I'm a big boy. I could have refused to take this trip with you."

Amy gazed into his blue eyes. The light in them held a potent message for her now. Already everything was changed between them. "You probably should have refused."

"Probably."

"What do we do now, Jack?"

"We do—" he paused and touched her cheek "—whatever you want."

"Why am I in charge?"

"Simple. If you keep treating me like a brother, I'll find the strength to act like one. But if you start treating me like a lover, I won't have the willpower to resist you. I'm only human, Amy."

"But you just said we have no future."

"That's right, but I discovered something a little while ago. When you're in my arms, the future doesn't matter to me anymore."

FOR THE REST of the afternoon Amy thought about what Jack had said, and by the time they returned to the hotel, she'd made a decision about how she would act once they were closed in that tiny room together again.

"I claim the shower first, big brother," she said gaily as she whisked in the door ahead of him. "Maybe I'll even leave a little hot water for you."

Jack stood perfectly still and watched her grab a sundress and underwear. "I see."

She paused and looked at him. "That's the best way, Jack. We'll hurt each other if we're not careful. I don't want that."

"Neither do I."

"Then it's settled."

Jack took the towel from around his neck and threw it on the bed. "Guess so, kid."

"Jack, you're not upset, are you?"

"Who, me?" He flashed her a grin. "Upset over some scrawny little thing who never did learn how to make a lay-up? Nah."

Amy crossed the room, her fist raised in the air. "Scrawny little thing? Jack Blickensderfer, I'll show—"

"Careful, Amy."

She stopped in midmotion at the warning.

"Don't touch right now, okay?" His blue eyes sent a chill down her spine.

"Okay." Without another word she retreated into the bathroom and closed the door. When she turned around, the first thing she saw was her lei in the sinkful of water, a silent reminder of Jack's thoughtfulness. He was quite a guy. And she was pushing him away. Amy had her hand on the bathroom door to go back into the room and tell Jack she'd made a mistake, when she heard him whistling.

How brokenhearted could he be if he was whistling? He sounded relieved and happy, not desolate. Amy took her hand away from the doorknob and began peeling off her wet bathing suit. She should be whistling, too. She'd won her trip to Hawaii, and tomorrow she'd see how fabulous her parents' property was. Right now Amy Hobson was on top of the world. Well, wasn't she?

The luau that was part of the trip package didn't fulfill all Amy's fantasies about such an event. Although the area set aside was within a hundred yards of the water, and blazing torches chased away the darkness, Amy was disappointed to discover that they were seated at long cafeteria-style tables set with normal plates, knives, forks and spoons.

"This seems so civilized," Amy whispered to Jack. "I thought we'd squat in a circle on the sand and eat out of communal bowls with our fingers."

He chuckled. "Have you by chance been reading James Michener recently?"

"Of course. I wanted to be informed."

"I hate to break it to you, Amy, but the islands have changed a little since the missionaries landed here. Most people use tables and chairs now."

"You're teasing me again."

"That's my job, kid."

She glanced sideways at him and caught a fleeting look of yearning before he turned away and picked up a small paper cup with something white in it.

"This isn't exactly a communal bowl, but you're supposed to use your fingers to taste this." He held the cup toward her.

"What is it?"

"Poi."

"Oh! I read about that, and I was hoping they'd have some here."

"Standard luau stuff," Jack said. "Dip your finger in and lick it off your finger. That's the only way to eat poi."

Amy poked her finger into the puddinglike mixture. "Feels like Elmer's Glue."

"Yep."

Amy licked her finger. "And it tastes like Elmer's Glue! Yuck! How did the natives ever enjoy this?"

"They were used to eating it, just like you're used to pizza. If you could transport a pizza back a hundred years and feed it to the villagers, they'd probably throw the whole thing to the dogs."

"Do you like poi, Jack?"

"Can't stand the stuff."

"Then why didn't you warn me?"

He took a sip of his rum-flavored mai-tai. "I may have warned you about too many things, Amy. Sometimes you have to find out for yourself what you like and don't like, what's good for you and what isn't."

Amy lowered her voice. "If you're talking about this afternoon, Jack, I'm glad you warned me about what might happen between us. And you should be, too."

"I am." He swallowed the last of his mai-tai. "I'm overjoyed. Now let's watch the dancing. You can pick up some pointers for your next hula contest."

Amy pressed her lips together. Obviously Jack was angry about their situation, but she was determined to carry through with her decision to keep her emotions, and therefore his, in check. To surrender to her feelings for Jack would make matters worse, not better.

The dancers were excellent, and one woman in particular seemed to catch Jack's interest. He leaned forward with his chin on his hands and watched the sensual sway of her hips while Amy clenched her teeth and tried not to care. She had no right to care, she told herself.

The drums began to give her a headache. Was she imagining things, or had the dancer become aware of Jack's interest? The woman seemed to be looking at Jack and smiling while she moved sensuously through her routine, and yes, Jack was smiling back at her!

Amy kicked him under the table. "What are you trying to do?" she whispered.

Jack continued to watch the dancer. "Make you jealous."

"Well, you're not succeeding!" She grabbed her mai-tai glass and drained it.

When the dance was finished the woman came down from the stage and walked over to Jack. "We need a volunteer from the audience for the next number," she said in a melodious voice. "I think you'd be perfect."

"Sure, why not?" Jack got up immediately and followed the woman.

Amy's eyes narrowed to slits. Now what? Jack's ogling the dancer had caused her to choose him to participate in the next number. What else had he begun with his flirting? Amy decided that perhaps she wouldn't have to worry about sleeping in the same room with Jack tonight. Maybe he'd be invited to spend the night elsewhere. And that would be fine and dandy with her. Yessiree.

The jovial host of the luau stepped to the microphone. "For the next number, one of our talented dancers has chosen someone from the audience to demonstrate how she can 'talk' with her body. In the old days a maiden communicated a great deal with her dancing."

The audience laughed, and the host continued his introduction.

"We'll see how well Lelani communicates with this young man by how easily he mimics her motions. An interesting way to say yes, wouldn't you agree?"

"No," Amy muttered to herself.

"But first let's find out a little about our fellow up here. Handsome devil, wouldn't you say, Lelani?"

The dancer nodded enthusiastically.

"What's your name, sir?" the host asked, thrusting a microphone at Jack.

"Jack Bond."

Amy noticed he used his radio name. Did he think that would sound more sexy to the dancer?

"And where are you from, Jack?"

"Bellingham, Washington."

"And what do you do in Bellingham besides drive the local ladies wild?"

Jack grinned knowingly. "That does take up quite a bit of my time, but I also spin a few records at KPLY."

"A disk jockey! I might have guessed something like that from the way you sidle up to a microphone. Well, Jack, you're already in communications, so I expect you'll be a whiz at communicating with this little lady."

"I'd sure like to try."

"That's the spirit! Music, please."

Amy wanted nothing more than to walk out on Jack, but that would be admitting that she was bothered by the sight before her. She was bothered, all right, but he would never know.

She pasted on a smile and focused directly on the stage as Jack began undulating in tune with the hula dancer's movements. When he lost the rhythm for a moment, the woman put her hands on his hips and guided him back in step. Amy gritted her teeth. If she hadn't thought of Jack as a sexual being before, she certainly did now. His suggestive movements brought whistles of approval from the audience.

Although Amy tried to tell herself that his performance disgusted her, that wasn't the emotion that brought a warm flush to her skin and a telltale ache deep within her. Amy knew that for her, the simple friendship she and Jack had once enjoyed was gone forever.

At the end of the dance the woman presented Jack with a flowered lei and kissed him. As Jack returned the kiss, Amy's control dissolved and she stood up to leave. She was almost out of the patio area when Jack caught up with her.

"Are we going home?" he asked, falling into step next to her.

"I don't know about you, but I am. After the way you communicated with the dancer back there, I figured you'd want to stay longer."

"Not really. If you're ready to go, that's fine with me."

Even without touching him, Amy felt surrounded by the warmth of his body, his musky scent. As they walked along the crowded street toward the hotel, Amy fought to erase the memory of his dance and the sensuous movements of his hips, but she couldn't forget. She had to get herself under control before they ended up in the hotel room together for an entire night.

Jack tipped his head back to glance at the night sky. "The moon's full. What about that stroll along the sand we talked about? Still interested?"

Amy marveled at his casual tone of voice. "Maybe . . . maybe that's a good idea."

"Then let's cut through here." He took her arm and guided her back toward the beach. His touch on her bare skin made her tremble, and he glanced down at her. "Cold?"

"Not really. I got a little sunburned this afternoon, that's all."

"Yeah, I noticed your cheeks are pink. Looks nice on you. Here, let's take off our shoes." He let go of her elbow and bent down to remove his Topsiders. He didn't touch her again as they stepped onto the beach and walked toward the water, carrying their shoes.

She almost wished that he would. His behavior was so offhand that Amy had trouble believing he was the same man who had kissed her that afternoon, or danced so erotically that night.

He sighed deeply. "Beautiful, isn't it?"

"Yes. Is that rain I feel?"

"Sure. Just a temporary little shower. There, see? It's over. We must have caught the edge of it."

Amy gazed up at the sky, where a few clouds scudded overhead, casting shadows on the sailboats moored offshore. The clouds moved quickly, and the boats were bathed in moonlight once again as they bobbed on the gentle waves.

"Jack, you'll think I'm crazy, but I see a rainbow in the sky over there." She pointed toward the horizon. "Except it's in shades of gray instead of colored. Am I imagining it?"

"No, you're not. That's a moonbow, Amy."

"A moonbow! This place is fantastic. I would have thought, once you saw Hawaii, that you would have wanted to move here, just like my father always has."

"Nope."

"Why not? You admit that it's beautiful." It occurred to Amy that if Jack would consider living in Hawaii, then perhaps their paths might not have to separate, after all. Maybe she wouldn't have to fight this yearning to turn and hold out her arms, to feel the length of his body pressed against hers.

"Hawaii is gorgeous, no doubt about it. Maybe that's part of the problem for me—not enough change. One monotonously beautiful day after another. I like the definite seasons, Amy. Autumn leaves and snow once in a while."

"Well, I've had enough of cold weather." His defense of Washington irritated her. Did he realize that he was cutting off any chance for their relationship to flourish? "This warm breeze feels heavenly to me and I love wearing a necklace made of fresh orchids. I can't imagine who wouldn't want to spend time in a paradise like this."

"Different strokes for different folks, Amy."

"We have completely different objectives, don't we, Jack?"

"So it seems."

"I made the right decision this afternoon."

He stopped walking. "Are you trying to convince yourself or me?"

"Both of us."

"Which means you're not totally convinced?"

"Yes, I'm convinced."

"You don't sound like it, Amy."

"I'm trying to sound like it." She twisted the strap of her sandal around one finger and stared down at the tiny sand hills and shadowed valleys created by hundreds of pairs of feet. "None of this helps, you know—moonlight, warm breezes, that hula you did..."

"Maybe I haven't really wanted to help."

She turned her gaze upward. "I should say not! I've never seen such a display in my life, Jack Blickensderfer."

His smile flashed white in the moonlight. "Now you know how I felt that day at the shopping mall."

Amy blinked. "But that was different. I wasn't deliberately seducing—"

"Tantalizing."

"What?"

"I wasn't seducing, I was tantalizing."

"Whatever you call it, you were coming on to that woman like nobody's business."

"Amy, that wasn't for her benefit. It was for yours."

"That's crazy." But she knew he was telling the truth.

"Can you blame me for wanting to show off a little, to see if I could get you to react? But I wasn't seducing you. Seductions require a closer range."

Amy's heart began a frantic pounding as he stepped forward. "Don't, Jack."

He toyed with the purple blossoms of her lei. "That didn't sound very convincing, either."

She worked to keep the quaver from her voice. "I mean it. I don't want this."

"Are you very sure?" He dropped his shoes to the sand and framed her face with both hands. "Your eyes say something else."

"No."

"Yes." His lips hovered nearer. "I want so much to love you."

She shivered at the caressing warmth of his magic voice. "Jack, if you're my friend, you won't do this."

"Haven't you realized?" His thumb traced the fullness of her bottom lip. "Our friendship is over, Amy." He covered her mouth with his and wrapped her in his arms. As he urged her against the hard wall of his chest, the air was filled with the delicate perfume of crushed orchids.

The moment their lips met, Amy's resistance to his kiss crumbled. No longer frightened by the sensual demand of his mouth and tongue, Amy was eager for his masculine assault. She tilted her head back and opened her lips to his invasion.

Jack was a heady combination of the known and the unknown, the strange and the familiar. Perhaps for that reason he brought with each touch a wild excitement that she'd never experienced before, not even with the man who had almost become her husband.

Her sandals fell from her limp fingers. As he deepened the kiss, she wound her arms around Jack's neck and buried both hands in his hair. Slowly Jack eliminated the space between them until their bodies connected, concave meeting convex in perfect symmetry.

He lightly grazed the side of her breast with one hand, and she moaned at the exquisite pleasure his touch gave her. Turning slightly, she pressed her hardened nipple against his palm. She longed for the thin material to be ripped away so that she could feel his skin against hers.

He lifted his head and gazed down at her as he cupped her aching breast. He was breathing hard. "I think . . . I think we'd better go somewhere else."

She smiled lazily. "Your place or mine?"

"Ours."

"Okay."

"Oh, Amy," he said with a sigh while he placed tiny kisses on her nose, lips and chin, "I never imagined Brad's little sister could be like this."

"Brad's little sister." Amy felt as if he'd thrown her in the ocean. The magic was gone.

7

JACK FELT HER STIFFEN. Damn! What had he said? Then he realized and groaned. "Amy, I'm sorry."

"Don't apologize." She twisted out of his embrace. "It's what you were thinking, isn't it?"

"I wasn't thinking, that's the point. You've always been Brad's little sister, and I guess the wonder of that came over me, the utter amazement that you've been around all these years and I've missed...we've missed—"

"And you reminded me of why none of this should be happening, Jack. We're heading in different directions, and we're going to get hurt. That kind of hurt spills over into other relationships, like yours and Brad's, for instance."

Jack rubbed the back of his neck. "Amy, why are we headed in different directions? Why do you have to follow your parents around?"

"Because they need me. I explained that."

"Then don't bring them to Hawaii."

"Jack, how can you ask me to be so selfish? Before Philip lost their savings, they always talked about living here. He destroyed their dream with my blessing, almost. I have to get it back."

"And sacrifice your own future?"

"What future? My big job at the lumberyard?"

"Dammit, Amy, I wasn't referring to your job, and you know it."

"Then what were you talking about? Am I supposed to give up all my plans on the strength of one kiss?"

"Of course not. But . . . oh, hell, maybe your parents do deserve to retire in Hawaii. Maybe you have to live near them for the rest of your life. But that boxes you in, Amy, and me out. That really frustrates me. I thought maybe if we could . . . if we had a chance to—"

"No," Amy said more gently. "That would only make matters worse. Come on, Jack. Let's go back to the room and get some sleep. Tomorrow's a busy day."

"Right. Sleep." He narrowed his eyes at her. "Are you going to be able to sleep after this?"

"I don't know. I'm going to try."

"How?"

She smiled. "I'll lie there and think of the time you put a rubber snake in my lunch box, and the day you called me 'peanut chest' in front of all your friends."

Jack squeezed his eyes shut. "Peanut chest. You don't qualify for that one anymore." He opened his eyes and gazed down at her. "You're so beautiful, Amy."

"Jack, I'm not that special. We got carried away by the moment, being here in Hawaii, on the beach with a full moon and the moonbow, and . . . everything."

"It was the everything that got me."

"No, the atmosphere of this place affected you. If we were back home, you'd still think of me as Brad's little sister."

He stood with his arms at his sides, gazing at her. "I doubt it. I think you'd still be a very sexy lady with a nonstop body and you'd test the virtue of a saint, which

I'm not. But somehow I'll try to forget you're sleeping in the same room with me tonight."

Amy bent to pick up her sandals. "Just remember the day I tape-recorded your romantic conversation with Jill Avery and played it the next time you came to our house for dinner."

Jack chuckled. "Ah, yes, so you did."

"And there was the afternoon I dropped your year-book in a mud puddle because you wouldn't take me skating."

"You were a little devil sometimes."

"Keep that in mind and you'll be fine."

"But you kiss like an angel, Amy Hobson."

Amy began retracing their path down the beach. "So do you, Jack Blickensderfer."

"Wait a minute. Then why—"

"Because we're both too smart to make a mistake like that," she said over her shoulder.

A short time later Jack stood under a very cold shower while Amy got ready for bed in the next room. He'd tried thinking of her as a little kid, as she'd suggested, but the mental image wouldn't stay when the voluptuous woman Amy had become was so close at hand. If he hadn't made that dumb remark about her being Brad's little sister, they'd be even closer right now.

But maybe she was right. They could both get hurt. Tomorrow she'd see her land purchase and the prospect of her moving to Hawaii would become a reality for both of them. That should make tomorrow night easier.

She'd dangled the possibility of his moving over here, too, but as tempting as he found Amy, the idea of running after her to Hawaii didn't appeal to him. This wasn't his choice of residence, and he wasn't sure about this tie she had with her parents, either. It seemed a little too tight for comfort.

When he began to shiver under the icy spray, Jack turned off the water and stepped out on the bath mat. After drying himself, he glanced around and realized he'd forgotten to bring clean undershorts into the bathroom. Deciding a draped towel was as modest as underwear, he tucked the white terry around his hips and walked out of the bathroom.

Amy was burrowed under the covers, with only her tousled dark hair visible. For a brief second Jack wondered what would happen if he crossed to her bed, slipped off his towel and climbed in with her. No. They had an agreement.

He pulled a clean pair of undershorts from the dresser drawer and walked to the far side of his bed before he sat down, unfastened the towel and put on the shorts.

Amy watched his progress with one eye uncovered. Under the heavy bedspread and sheets she was beginning to perspire, both from the weight of the covers and the sight of Jack wearing only a towel. How would he react if she tossed back the sheets and held out her arms to him? No. They'd made a deal.

She figured out what he was doing, and although she felt like a spy, she didn't look away when he removed the towel and stood up to finish putting on the underwear. He had a firm, muscled backside with a faint line where his bathing suit ended, a reminder of their two hours in the sun this afternoon. Amy licked dry lips. Well, she'd seen all there was to see of Jack except for . . . but she mustn't think about that.

Jack tossed back his covers and climbed into bed. As soon as he faced her, Amy closed her eyes and pretended to be asleep. She heard him click off the bedside lamp that rested on the table between them.

"Good night, Amy," he said in his best radio voice. She didn't answer.

"No matter what happens, I don't regret tonight."

Amy thought about the passionate kiss on the beach. She didn't regret it, either, but if she said so, if she indicated in any way that she was lying there wide awake, they might end up in the same bed yet. She kept her silence, and soon she heard Jack's even breathing. Contrary to what he'd proclaimed earlier about not being able to relax in the same bedroom with her, he appeared to be fast asleep.

BY ELEVEN the next morning they had flown to the neighboring island of Maui, and Jack was maneuvering their economy rental car along the twisting road leading to Hana, a town on the opposite side of the island from the airport.

"Jack, this is fantastic," Amy murmured. The narrow road hugged the coastline, giving them spectacular views of ocean-washed cliffs on their left and dense tropical growth on their right. "Pure Michener. I bet if you cut through those trees and vines you'd find an abandoned native village and stone idols lying around."

"Could be."

"Look, a waterfall! No, don't look," she amended as a truck thundered toward them and Jack had to swerve to the shoulder of the road to provide enough room for both vehicles. "This isn't fair, Jack. I'll drive on the way back so you can play tourist."

"Hey, enjoy yourself. I've been to Hawaii before, remember?"

"Yes, but you've never driven to Hana, right?"

Jack grimaced as the car hit a pothole. "Never had the pleasure. Amy, will your parents have to navigate this road often?"

"Oh, not much, probably. I hope not, anyway. It's not exactly an easy drive, is it?"

"Nope." Jack slowed the car to edge past a large van full of sightseers coming from Hana.

"But that's why the area's so special. Lots of celebrities have homes near Hana."

"Celebrities can afford helicopters."

"Okay, so the road is a disadvantage, but Mom and Dad will be so happy in their place by the ocean they won't want to leave very often. Besides, they'll be retired. They can drive this route as slowly as they want to. We're the ones on a schedule."

"You're right, Amy. If we had the whole day to spend getting there, we could stop along the way, maybe have a picnic by one of those waterfalls."

Amy glanced at him. "Yes, we could." Immediately she thought of what else they could do, hidden from public view by the lush foliage. A picnic on a soft blanket. A basket of Hawaii's famous fruit—golden pineapple, kiwi, mangoes and papayas—and maybe some crab legs dipped in a tangy sauce and a bottle of Chablis chilled under the waterfall. And then, after the picnic, they could stretch out on the soft blanket and . . .

"Yo, Amy. Come in, Amy."

She returned to reality with a start. "Did you say something, Jack?"

"Just that we're approaching Hana and I need my navigator to help me find the development office."

"Oh." Amy fumbled in her purse and took out a map. "Sorry. I was daydreaming."

"About what?"

"Um, not much. Take the next left turn."

From her refusal to answer him directly, Jack concluded that Amy's daydreaming had something to do with him. And that was only fair, after the kind of dreams he'd had last night. Instead of lying awake thinking of Amy, he'd gone right to sleep, which might have been worse. When his subconscious had taken over, it presented him with a vision of Amy as a brown-skinned native girl wearing only a grass skirt and a deep pink lei that brushed the tips of her swaying breasts as she danced for him.

After the dance she drew him into the privacy of her grass hut. His fingers trembled as he unfastened the flimsy skirt and gently pushed her down on the woven mat. The lei nestled in the valley between her breasts, and he inhaled its fragrance as his mouth captured—

"Left, Jack, left!" Amy shook his arm. "Oh, now you've missed the turn. We'll have to go back."

He stepped on the brakes, checked for traffic and swung the car around. Would she ask what he'd been thinking about so intently? If she did, he might tell her just to get her reaction. But she didn't ask and he felt a pang of disappointment.

The development office was located in a mobile home on a cleared plot of land. Green indoor-outdoor carpeting covered the wooden steps leading up to the door, which was propped open. A round-faced jovial man rose from behind the desk as Amy and Jack stepped into the makeshift office.

"Good morning! Can I show you folks a lot today? They're going like hotcakes, but we still have a few choice parcels left—a couple right by the beach, or if you prefer inland a little ways, we—"

"Thank you, but I've already bought a lot. I'm here to see it."

"Indeed?" The man's smile lost some of its luster. "And your name?"

"Amy Hobson. I bought the lot by mail. I'm from Washington."

"Excellent, excellent." The man walked to a gray file cabinet and pulled out a middle drawer. "Here we are," he said, picking out a file and opening it. "Lot number two, is that right?"

Amy nodded with relief. In the back of her mind she'd always wondered if perhaps the land was some sort of hoax and that she'd been defrauded again. "That's right. Down by the beach. We'd like directions."

"Okay. Here's where you go." The man picked up a well-sharpened pencil and drew a rough map on a pad of paper, explaining the landmarks as he went. When he was finished he tore the paper from the pad and handed it to Amy.

Jack glanced around the small office. "So you do quite a bit of business here?"

"Actually, today's a little slow. A weekday, you know. Things pick up on the weekends."

Jack looked skeptical. "Do lots of people travel that road?"

The man laughed. "It's a pistol, isn't it? But that's what you want when you buy a spot to get away from it all. You don't want a location that's easy for everyone to find. Spoils the seclusion."

"Hmm."

"Let's go, Jack. I can hardly wait to see where my parents are going to spend their golden years." Amy started out the door.

Jack turned back for a moment to the man behind the desk. "She's buying this lot for her parents, for their retirement."

"Is she? Well, a lot of corporate types love this area after the hustle and bustle of the business world."

"How many have their own helicopters?"

"A few. Others have small planes hangared at our little local airport. Some people who don't like to fly and don't care for the drive just hire someone to go into Wailuku to stock up on groceries. We have a small market here, but all the major shopping is on the other side of the island."

"Hmm."

"Jack," Amy called from the steps outside. "Are you coming or not?"

"Be right there." He looked at the man again. "Is there a resale clause with these contracts?"

"Resale? You mean some guarantee that we'll buy it back or something?"

"Right."

"No, I'm afraid not. But nobody's ever wanted that. This is paradise, mister, and they all want a piece of it."

"I see. Well, I guess we're off to see the piece of paradise she's staked a claim to. Aloha." With a slight nod Jack left the office. He found Amy standing at the edge of the clearing, gazing up in wonder at a plant that towered several feet above her.

"Bananas, Jack, growing right on this tree! Mom and Dad can grow tropical fruit in their own backyard."

"They may have to if they want to eat," Jack muttered as they returned to the car.

"What did you say?"

Jack waited until they were inside the car before answering. He hated so much to rain on her parade. "Amy, unless your parents can afford to have someone shop for them, they'll have to take that road around to Wailuku every time they buy a big supply of groceries."

"Is that what the man said?"

"In effect, yes."

"Then I'll drive it for them."

"That's the other thing bothering me, Amy. Hana is a small place. Where will you find a job here?"

"I—I didn't think I'd be limited just to Hana."

"You're limited by that road. I can't imagine working somewhere else on the island and taking that monster trip back home every day."

"Then I'll have to find a job here, won't I? Because this is going to work out, Jack. I'll make it work out."

"I sure hope you can, Amy."

"I will. Now let's go find my lot."

As they followed the salesman's directions to the development site, Amy took note of the area around her. "I see what you mean, Jack. Hana isn't exactly a metropolitan hub, is it?"

"My guess is that it's home to pioneer types and rich people."

"And you're thinking that my parents don't fit in either category."

"That's what I'm thinking."

"Wait'll we get to the beach. Think of it, Jack, a home right next to the beach. That's worth putting up with a few disadvantages, in my opinion."

"Maybe so."

Within five minutes Amy scrambled out of the car and stood staring in dismay at the sight before her. "What's wrong with the sand, Jack? Why is it black?"

He scratched the back of his neck. "Well, Hawaii has some black sand beaches, now that I think of it. I guess this is one of them."

"Black sand? I never heard of such a thing!"

He heard the despair in her voice and put a comforting arm around her. "Don't you think it's kind of exotic? Maybe your folks will love this. And the water is beautiful, Amy. They'll have a terrific view. Look at how the waves crash over those rocks." He squeezed her shoulder. "It's a dramatic spot you've bought."

"Black sand," Amy wailed forlornly. "I never thought to ask if the beach had the right color of sand. I've seen pictures of Maui. They didn't look like this."

"You probably saw shots of Kaanapali, where most of the resorts are. That's a different part of the island. Amy, do you think their advertisements misled you? If so, we can take some action. If they showed you pictures of Kaanapali, and yet were selling this land—"

"No, they didn't. I made that connection on my own. They described this as waterfront property on Maui near Hana. It was a small ad, with no pictures. People in the know would have realized the beaches were black."

"Amy, I'm sure many people consider this a plus. Not many people live near such an unusual phenomenon."

"And neither will my parents! I've heard my father talk about how he loved the wide stretches of clean white sand. That's the Hawaii he remembers, and I know he wouldn't like this. I just know it."

He gave her a little shake. "I think you should give them a chance to see it before making that choice."

"No. I can picture their faces, the disappointment written all over them. Besides, you've had reservations about this place ever since we drove that road. You're right, Jack. Rich people, people who crave something different and secluded, belong here. And then there are the adventurous ones, the pioneer types you talked about. But for Mom and Dad I want the Hawaii on all the travel posters. I blew it, Jack."

"This lot is probably still an excellent investment."

"Maybe, but I'm going back to the salesman and ask him to sell it for me. I can't afford investments. I've got to unload this and try again."

Jack winced. After what the man had said, Amy's chances of getting him to take the property for resale weren't good. But then again, Amy Hobson wasn't the sort of person to stay down for the count. Maybe she could swing a deal.

AS IT TURNED OUT, Amy couldn't, and Jack let her vent her frustration in an angry tirade that lasted through most of the tortuous drive back to the airport and even spilled over into the short plane ride to Oahu.

"We've got one day left," Amy said grimly as they returned to their hotel room. "We'll spend it covering every real estate office in Honolulu until we find someone willing to list that property. I'm selling it, and that's final." She flopped down on her bed.

"But what about your plan?"

"My plan's down the toilet, Jack. At least I want my money back so I can try again someday."

"Maybe you could find something else while we're running around to the real estate companies." He wondered why he was suggesting any alternatives. If he left everything alone, Amy's Hawaiian dreams might fizzle out completely. Then they'd have time to explore the feelings they had for each other.

"I thought of that, but one day isn't long enough, and besides, I can't afford to pay on two pieces of property. I have to sell this one before I can start over."

"Maybe some company would be willing to work a swap."

"Maybe, but that's a long shot and you know it. Besides, I'm not buying anything in haste. No way do I want to get burned a second time." She laughed without humor. "Or I should say a third time. What a bozo I am."

"No, you're not, Amy. That's a prize piece of land you bought. It's just not right for your folks, that's all." Jack stood with his hands in his pockets, gazing across the room at the picture she made sprawled on the bed, a dejected beauty in white slacks and a pale green sleeveless sweater that had inched up over her waist to reveal a strip of white skin.

He doubted that she had any self-awareness at the moment. She didn't realize that as she lay there with her hands flung out at her sides, she seemed to be issuing an invitation for him to lie beside her and kiss that tiny strip of exposed skin.

Arousal pulsed through him, hot and heavy. And what was to stop them now? Amy's plans for her parents were on hold and perhaps never would reach fruition. He wondered if Amy understood yet what that could mean to them. Probably not. She was too caught up in regret about her parents. He'd wait a little while and let the truth of their new circumstances dawn upon her slowly, so he wouldn't startle her. But he didn't intend to wait all night.

"Feel like walking over to the International Marketplace?" he asked. "We could get something to eat."

Amy sighed. "I'm not very hungry, but I imagine you're starved."

"Uh-huh." And not for food, either, he amended silently.

"We might as well." She stood up and walked to the dresser to find her hairbrush. "Real estate offices aren't open at night, and we have to pass the time somehow."

"That's true." Jack looked away, afraid she'd read in his expression exactly how he wanted to pass the time until morning.

The International Marketplace was, like most of Honolulu, a blur of activity and color. A huge, wizened old banyan tree strung with lights formed the hub of the market, which included dozens of open-air stalls and shops selling articles from all over the world. Numerous restaurants, serving both Polynesian and Oriental food, dotted the marketplace. Amy and Jack sampled some of both as they strolled through the carnival atmosphere.

"I think you should have one of these," Jack said, fingering the silky material of a pink-and-white flowered sarong. "Let me buy it for you."

"That's silly, Jack. We're not here to pick up souvenirs."

He unhooked the hanger from the rack and held the garment up to her. "Terrific."

"No, Jack."

"Look, this isn't a knickknack that would collect dust. You could wear it."

"In Bellingham, where the temperature seldom gets above seventy-five?"

"I thought you planned to live in Hawaii someday."

She looked up at him. "That's nice of you to say, Jack. At least someone still believes in me. But I don't know how soon I'll get here. It could be years. In the meantime that sarong would go to waste."

"Just step over to the mirror and see how nice it looks. Here." He thrust the garment at her.

"Oh, all right, if you insist, but we're not buying anything, Jack." She took the bright material and gathered it against her as she stood in front of a long mirror.

Jack came up behind her and caught her gaze in the mirror. "See how it makes your eyes sparkle?"

"That's the lights from the banyan tree." Amy wondered if he knew that any sparkle he noticed was generated by his being so close behind her. One step back and she'd be in his arms.

"I'm going to buy it. You can wear it around your apartment, as sort of a lounging outfit, and . . ."

"And what?"

"And . . ." He paused and gazed directly into her eyes. "When I see you in it, I'll remember this trip."

His implication that he'd be at her apartment often startled her. Her disappointment that day had been so severe that it had blotted out all her thoughts of the future—but not Jack's, evidently. Her heart began to hammer and her smile trembled at the corners. "After all the crummy experiences I've put you through, I can't imagine why you'd want to remember this trip."

His voice was soft. "Can't you?"

A thrill of awareness traveled up her spine, and she tilted her head to one side to look at him in the mirror. "Jack?"

He took her by the shoulders and turned her around to face him. When he spoke, it was in a tone so low that only she could hear him. "You said yourself that you may never move here."

"That's . . . that's true."

"Then—" His blue gaze searched her face and his grip on her shoulders tightened possessively. "There's no reason to sleep in separate beds tonight, Amy."

8

AMY STARED AT HIM. "I guess you're right."

"Take the sarong." Desire shimmered in his blue eyes. "Wear it for me tonight."

Nervous excitement clogged Amy's throat, choking off her reply. She understood what he was suggesting, that in the privacy of their hotel room she come to him clothed in the sarong . . . and nothing else.

"Stay right here," he instructed, taking the sarong from her. "I'll pay for it."

Amy wound both arms around her rib cage and tried to control her trembling as Jack sought the clerk and handed over the money for the dress. Unless Amy stopped him, she and Jack were destined to spend the night in each other's arms. She shivered with passion and a touch of fear.

Once they'd made love, she would lose her protective, brotherly friend forever. But the magic of his kiss promised a passionate experience unlike anything she'd ever known. The stakes were high. Was she ready to risk a friend to find a lover?

He walked back to her, a plastic bag containing the sarong in one hand, his blue eyes focused intently on her face. "Second thoughts?" he murmured, guiding her out of the shop.

"Jack, this is scary."

"Change always is."

"What if we're terrible together? Then we'll have ruined everything."

A hint of a smile touched his lips as he glanced down at her. "Terrible?" He shook his head. "Loving you couldn't possibly be terrible. Not for me. And I'll try not to make you miserable in the process, either."

She couldn't help chuckling. "I doubt if you could do that."

"I've managed in the past."

"That's different."

"Yes." He wrapped his free arm securely around her waist. "And so are we. We might as well face the fact."

Amy's laugh was slightly giddy. "And make the best of it?"

"I think that's exactly what we're about to do. At long last." He quickened his pace.

"Jack, you're almost running."

"That's right. I would run if I didn't think some cop would suspect me of having stolen something. We've wasted too much time already."

"We've only been here two days."

"Two very long days. Or am I the only one who's been in torment around here?"

She glanced up at his sharply defined profile, the high forehead, long dark lashes, straight nose. And his mouth—wide and generous when he smiled in friendship, but able to arouse the most primitive instincts in her with a single kiss. Torment? Amy guessed that was a pretty good word to describe what she'd been through in the past two days.

"Come on, Amy, boost my ego." They paused for a traffic light and he bent to whisper in her ear. "You've been hot for my body, too. Admit it."

. "Just a little."

"Going to play it cool, are you?"

"Maybe."

"That's what you think." He gripped her tighter as they walked into the deserted hotel lobby. The crowds were on the streets and in the shops and restaurants at this time of the evening. Jack punched the elevator button and they stood alone before the beige metal doors.

"And what's that supposed to mean, Jack?"

"It means that I'm not holding back tonight, and if I have anything to say about it, neither will you."

Excitement washed over her in alternately hot and cold waves. "Is that right?" she teased, watching passion brighten his blue eyes.

"That's right." The ping of the elevator placed an exclamation mark after his statement. As the doors slid open on the empty cubicle he drew her inside and pushed the eighth-floor button. When the doors closed again, he backed her against the paneled elevator wall and slid his hand beneath her hair to caress the nape of her neck. "I'm going to love you until you can't see straight," he murmured, and brought his lips down on hers.

The thrust of his tongue had more meaning now, and as he stroked the inside of her mouth, Amy's body responded with a rush of warmth that settled into an exquisite, aching pulse between her thighs. Jack brushed his pelvis across hers, and she put her hands on his hips to mold him closer to the source of her heat.

When he lifted his head, his soft laughter held a trace of masculine pride. "So you've been interested in me just a little, Amy?"

"More than that."

"How much?"

"Right now?"

"Yes." He pressed the hardness of his groin against her. "Right now."

"I'm going crazy inside, Jack," she admitted breathlessly.

His voice was husky. "That makes two of us." At the rumble of the elevator doors he glanced up at the lighted numbers. "We're home." He hugged her swiftly and released her to reach in his pocket for the room key.

Amy's heartbeat seemed extraordinarily loud to her as they walked down the silent, carpeted hallway with Jack's arm still possessively tucked around her waist, as if he feared she might run away. In some ways she wanted to. But then she would never know what it felt like to be loved by Jack. And she longed to know.

Jack turned the key in the lock and within seconds had the door closed behind them. They were alone.

He tilted her face up to his. "I'd like it very much if you'd go into the bathroom and put the sarong on."

Amy nodded, not trusting herself to speak. She took the bag from him and turned toward the bathroom.

He reached out and caught her arm. "But before you go, I want to tell you something, just so you won't worry, in case you haven't, uh . . ."

She turned back to him with a questioning glance.

"Amy, this may sound like I planned everything, but so that you know—" He paused. "I've taken care of birth control."

"Oh." Amy flushed. In her concern about the psychological effects of making love to an old friend, she'd forgotten about the physical ones. But Jack hadn't forgotten. In fact, he'd apparently thought about it before they left Washington.

"I could pretend that I make a habit of packing condoms in my suitcase, but that wouldn't be true, and besides, you'd think something worse of me, as if I usually—"

"Are you saying that you . . . brought them because of me?"

"Yes."

Amy looked at him steadily. "Then you did plan this."

"Not exactly. I hoped for this."

"When did you start hoping, Jack? How long have you thought of me as . . . as more than Brad's little sister?"

"For quite a while. My image of you hasn't been the same ever since you danced at the mall." He caressed the inside of her elbow with his thumb. "I've tried to keep my brotherly attitude toward you, but I've biffed that miserably. It seems that you turn me on, Amy Hobson."

"You mean, all this time that we've been working with Steve and Beeper, you've—"

"Wanted to hold you, love you, run my hands all over your body. Yes, Amy. I've wanted to take off every stitch and kiss you everywhere. I've wanted to be inside you and feel your softness closing around me."

Amy's voice came out as a tremulous whisper. "I didn't know."

"I didn't want you to know. You were moving as soon as possible to Hawaii. But now that your plans have changed, so has everything else." He swallowed. "And if you don't get in there and put on that sarong right now, I'll be a crazy man."

Without a word she turned away and walked into the bathroom. She was reeling from the knowledge that Jack had kept his emotions bottled up for so many weeks. Weeks of wanting her. Would she be a disappointment to him? She didn't want to be, but Philip was the only lover she'd ever had, and he hadn't raved about how wonderful she was in bed.

Amy fumbled with her clothes. Maybe she and Jack should forget the whole thing. His fantasies would stay intact. Clad only in her underwear, she sat on the edge of the tub and gazed at the white tile under her bare feet. She sensed that Jack was experienced with women, no matter how much he protested that he didn't carry birth control around with him all the time.

At first his admission of desire had excited her, but as the minutes ticked by she found his anticipation an overwhelming burden. She couldn't possibly be as terrific as he expected, and then he'd regret that they'd ever made love. But he would continue to be kind, because of their past friendship, and he'd try to let her down easily. Amy didn't think she could stand Jack's pity.

"Amy?" He knocked on the door. "Are you all right? You're very quiet in there."

"I'm . . . I'm thinking."

His muttered exclamation was indecipherable through the door, but she stood up in alarm when the knob turned.

"I'm coming in."

Amy grabbed the pink-and-white sarong and held it in front of her as he stepped through the door. He'd taken off his shirt, and she couldn't help gazing at the muscled beauty of his chest.

His glance flicked slowly over her. "What is it, Amy?"

She looked away from the Grecian perfection of his body. His magnificence only intimidated her more. "I've decided this is a mistake."

He didn't touch her, but his voice was like velvet brushing against her skin. "Why?"

"I think you've built me into some sort of goddess, and I'm not. I'm just me, Amy Hobson, Brad's little sister. I'm not very exciting, Jack."

He looked at her standing there with one slim leg covered by the sarong and the other exposed to his view right up to the white lace of her sexy little panties, and thought he'd never seen anyone more exciting in his life. Only the sarong and two wisps of easily removed material separated him from caressing every intimate part of her with his hungry gaze, and his mouth went dry at the thought.

"You're older than I am, Jack, and very—" She glanced at him but forced her attention away again as the thrust of his aroused body against the fabric of his slacks heated the blood in her veins. "Very good-looking," she finished quickly. "I imagine you've been to bed with lots of women, and making love to me won't be any different, really. We should just skip it and try to keep what's left of our friendship." But she wondered how she'd ever lapse into easy friendship again. Fool that she was, she wanted him even more now than before.

He searched frantically for the right words, the words that would allay her fears and bring her to him. "I don't expect a goddess, Amy. I expect a flesh-and-blood woman, someone who's not afraid to let her passion show, to want me as much as I want her. Amy, can't you understand that technique and experience don't matter? What matters is yearning, desire, even lust. I've seen all those in your eyes."

Her mouth parted and her breathing became quick and shallow. He decided to go for broke. "Touch me, Amy."

"Jack—"

"Touch me."

"No." Even as she shook her head she took a step toward him.

"Yes. Come closer, Amy."

Like a sleepwalker, she took another step forward.

Jack reached for her wrist and the sarong fell to the tiled floor. Gently he guided her hand to its destination and closed his eyes as the grasp of her smooth fingers threatened to send him over the edge.

At the same moment that he heard her intake of breath she removed her hand, but when he looked into her eyes the brown depths were blazing with the same need that was slowly turning him inside out. Still grasping her wrist, he kept his gaze locked with hers as he led her into the other room and over to his bed.

He reached to unhook her bra before slowly drawing the straps over her arms and tossing the garment to the floor. Then he deliberately lowered his gaze as his hand curved naturally beneath the satin underside of one breast. He could almost believe that the length and breadth of his fingers had been measured for just this purpose, to gently nudge the pouting tip upward to his waiting lips.

She trembled as he pulled the firm bud into his mouth and began to suck gently. He felt dizzy with the pleasure of tasting her at last, and his legs began to shake. He wondered what kind of control he'd have left by the time he entered her. Maybe none.

She pushed her fingers through his hair and urged him closer. Her moan as he nipped her with his teeth made his blood sing. She was catching up with him, and soon she would match his turbulent emotion.

The quivering in his legs became worse, and he released her for a moment to discard his slacks and briefs. Then he urged her back onto the bed. With one swift movement he took away her panties and discovered that the silken fabric was drenched with her moisture. "Yes," he whispered fiercely, crushing the garment in one fist and daring her to meet his gaze. "Now you understand what I've been going through."

"Jack," she breathed, closing her eyes and arching her body against the sheets. "Oh, Jack."

"Look at me, Amy."

Her lashes fluttered open, and her brown eyes were glazed with passion.

"And you thought you wouldn't be special," he murmured, laying his palm against the flat plane of her stomach. "This is special." He moved his hand lower, past the thicket of dark curls until his fingers caressed the damp, fragrant place her body had created to welcome him.

At his touch she cried out, and he kissed the cry from her lips as he continued to stroke her until she writhed on the bed in a tangle of sheets. He knew that once she was under him, he would be ready to explode, and he wanted her to be that way, too.

Amy clenched her lower lip between her teeth as the tension built to an unbearable level. She wanted to beg him to fill her, but her words had become moans and animal sounds that she didn't recognize. She couldn't think anymore, could barely see him through the haze of desire that gripped her. Never had she known such wanting. Never.

Then she felt the stir of air as he moved away and opened the bedside table drawer. Seconds later he returned and she looked up into his face, a face that reflected the same agony of waiting that tormented her heated body. "Please," she whispered, and with a moan he buried his throbbing shaft deep inside her.

She lifted her hips to push against him and he answered her, initiating a feverish rhythm that wrenched breathless cries from her lips. At last, with one final thrust, he set off the violent tremors that rocked them both in a passionate cradle of completion.

Many long minutes later, the chill from the open lanai door forced Jack to roll reluctantly away from her and reach for the sheet at the bottom of the bed. As he drew it over her flushed skin, she stirred and opened her eyes.

He smiled down at her. "I thought you might be asleep."

"No chance."

"Oh? And what's that supposed to mean?"

"I think sleep is a waste of time," she said with a lazy grin. "How about you?"

"Couldn't agree more."

"Then you're not terribly disappointed in Brad's little sister?" She was proud of herself that she could treat the subject lightly now. And why not? For the first time in her life she felt like a woman, not somebody's little sister.

"You know I'm not disappointed. Only a stupid person would think what we just shared was even remotely disappointing, and you're not stupid."

"Thank you."

"Or undersexed."

"Do I thank you for that remark, too?"

"No. I thank you for being such a hot-blooded wench. But I'm not surprised. Anybody who would crawl down a movie theater aisle for the fun of it has a real zest for life."

"You really think you know me, don't you, Jack?"

"I think I'd like to get to know you better," he said with a leer as he pulled the cover away from her rosy breasts.

By the next morning, they knew each other very well.

"I wish we didn't have to spend all day visiting real estate offices," Amy complained as she bit into a slice of papaya from the breakfast tray Jack had ordered.

"You're insatiable, and I love it."

"How do you know that's what I meant? Maybe I wanted to visit Pearl Harbor and Diamond Head today."

"Sure you did."

"You have a high opinion of your charms if you think I'd want to spend the last full day of my Hawaiian trip in a hotel room making love to you." At his crestfallen look she took pity on him. "But if we didn't have to tour the real estate offices, that's exactly what I'd want to do," she said softly.

His smile returned full force. "I knew it all the time."

"No, you didn't, but you should. You're a wonderful lover, Jack. And it's positively criminal that we have to take our time for the real estate business."

"You're good for my ego, Amy. Maybe we'll find someone right away who wants to list your land. We could, you know."

"That's true. No matter what that silly salesman said about nobody wanting to touch it. He could be wrong. In fact, he probably was trying to discourage me from selling. I made my payments regularly, and he doesn't want to lose me."

Jack's expression grew serious. "Neither do I. Promise me that this isn't just a shipboard romance, Amy."

"How can it be? We're not even on a boat."

"You know what I mean. You won't ditch me once we're back in Washington, will you?"

"I might ask you the same thing, Jack."

"Fair enough. I plan to be camped on your doorstep every free moment I have. Does that answer your question?"

Amy shrugged. "I suppose if you insist on staying out there, I can't force you to come inside and share my nice warm apartment, or my nice warm bed, or my nice warm—"

"Whoa." Jack took a deep breath and stood up. "Cut the vivid descriptions or we won't make it out of here this morning."

"You're weak, Jack."

"Yes, ma'am, I certainly am."

Amy licked the papaya juice from her fingers while she gazed up at him in seeming innocence.

"Amy Hobson, I'm warning you."

"Wonderful breakfast, Jack. I was expecting peanut butter sandwiches to go."

"And Lord knows what you would have done with peanut butter," he said hoarsely. "Would you please stop that and finish getting ready?"

"If you insist." Amy wandered into the bathroom to brush her teeth and put on the last of her makeup. Jack's heartfelt sigh followed her, and she laughed happily.

When he walked into the bathroom a few minutes later, he appeared to have regained control as he leaned nonchalantly against the counter while she applied her lipstick. She turned to him with a smile. "Better now?"

"I'm learning the necessary art of restraint."

"I shouldn't tease you."

"Don't ever stop, Amy. It's the sweetest torture I've ever known."

"What a nice thing to say. But I have to remember you make your living being glib, Jack Bond."

"Jack Bond didn't make love to you last night."

"He didn't?"

"No. That was me, Amy."

She gazed into his blue eyes. "I'm glad."

"Me too." He paused. "I can't get over how natural it feels to share a living space with you."

"That's understandable. We practically grew up together." She recapped her tube of lipstick.

"Yeah." He chuckled. "It seems funny now to think back over those years and compare them with the past few hours. But maybe all that time, all that history, is what made last night so special."

"I think so." Amy looked directly at him and they stared at each other for a long moment.

"I wasn't kidding, Amy. I don't want to lose you."

"After last night, you'd have to pry me away with a crowbar."

"That's good to hear." He pushed away from the counter and took her hand. "Come on, let's go find out about your land. For all we know, the first real estate agent we talk to will agree to list it, and we'll be free for the rest of the trip."

By late afternoon Jack's optimism was almost funny for Amy to recall. But she didn't feel like laughing. They'd combed Oahu searching for a real estate company interested in Amy's land, and always the answer was the same.

"The resale market on that development is dead until all the lots are gone and people have started to build," one agent explained patiently. "Come back in two or three years, and you'll have something worth peddling. Until then it's not worth my time or yours, unless you want to take a big loss."

"I can't afford a big loss." Amy's shoulders slumped.

"Then I advise you to hold on to your property. The development hasn't caught on yet, but it will. These things take time. You've got a good investment, and you bought when prices were still low. Sit tight and you'll have a bonanza."

"But I don't want the lot anymore, and I can't wait several years to sell it," Amy protested.

"I wish I could help you, but my sales force couldn't move that lot with a forklift." The man stood up and held out his hand. "Good luck to both of you. You're not by chance honeymooning in Hawaii, are you?"

Amy glanced at Jack and found him watching her with an amused expression. "No," she said, releasing the man's hand at once. "We're just . . . friends."

"I see." The agent shook hands with Jack. "My mistake. We get a lot of newlyweds over here." He laughed and shook his head. "Although I don't know why they waste the money. My friends in the hotel business tell me the couples arrive, take one perfunctory trip to the beach, and never come out of their rooms again. They might as well have stayed in St. Louis, or wherever they're from."

Amy flushed and looked down at the beige carpet. If the honeymooners had as much fun as she and Jack did in their hotel room, she could understand why sightseeing would lose its appeal.

Jack cleared his throat. "If either of us ever considers Hawaii for a honeymoon, we'll keep that in mind."

The agent winked. "Don't tell the Chamber of Commerce I said so, but my advice is to wait until you've been married for twenty years or so. Then you can dispense with all that romantic stuff and truly appreciate the beauty of the islands."

"I see what you mean," Jack said, and winked back. "I remember some prediction about beans in a jar."

"Uh-huh."

"Well, take it easy, Mr. Rodenberry."

"You too—both of you. And good luck."

When they were back on the sidewalk, Amy poked Jack in the ribs. "What beans in a jar? What sort of little men's joke were you two sharing?" Jack laughed and Amy poked him again. "What's so funny? And where do you get off agreeing with him that after twenty years or so you can 'dispense with all that romantic stuff'? Answer me, Jack Blickensderfer!"

"Ow, my poor ribs!" He chuckled and slipped an arm around her waist. "Haven't you heard the 'beans in a jar' theory of married sex?"

"Absolutely not."

"Someone, and I can't remember who, once said that if a couple put a bean in a jar for every time they made love the first year they were married, and took one out every time from then on, they'd never empty the jar."

"That's ridiculous."

"I agree."

"You do?"

"Completely." He gazed down into her face. "If a man had someone like you around, he'd empty that jar in no time." A soft light shone in his eyes. "Tell me, are you into disproving theories?"

Amy's indignation faded as she absorbed the meaning of his question. "Jack, I—"

"Okay, we'll shelve that particular discussion until later. But it doesn't look as if you're going to sell that land, Amy. Not anytime soon."

"I think you're right." Her land scheme for her parents wasn't working out at all. But there was always a flip side, as Jack had said. Without the threat of moving to Hawaii, her future with Jack was sparkling with promise.

"Hey, I have an idea." Jack stopped beside a sidewalk souvenir stand and picked out a bright pink Frisbee decorated with palm trees and hula dancers. "Come on," he said, paying for the Frisbee and leading her across the busy street to a grassy park. "We need to loosen up."

"Jack," Amy protested with a laugh. "I haven't played Frisbee since—"

"Since you and Brad and I used to play on the street in front of your house, right?"

"I guess that's right."

"It'll come back to you," Jack called over his shoulder as he jogged several feet away. "Catch." With an expert twist of his wrist he sent the round plastic disk whirling in her direction.

"You're a crazy man." Amy dropped her purse and snagged the Frisbee out of the air as if she'd been practicing for weeks.

"All right, Amy!" Jack whooped and shot his fist in the air. Then he started to jog backward. "Let's see you toss it this far, expert."

Amy flung the pink disk in a high arc toward him. The motion felt great, as if she were sending her troubles sailing away into the blue Hawaiian sky along with the bright Frisbee.

Jack leaped to catch it, and Amy took pleasure in the agile movement of his body. She'd always loved to watch him, she realized now, even when they were kids and she hadn't quite understood the fascination he held for her.

"Coming at you," Jack called, and whipped the Frisbee from behind his back.

"Show-off," Amy taunted as she dashed for the flying disk. She missed and landed with a soft thud in the grass.

"Oh, no. Amy go boom," Jack said, running to her aid. He knelt beside her. "I hope nothing's hurt."

Amy chuckled. "Just my pride. I wanted to prove I was still up to the challenge."

"You are." He grinned at her. "You can still throw a mean Frisbee, lady."

"Brings back memories of the good old days, doesn't it?"

Jack held out his hand and helped her up. "Those weren't the good old days. These are."

"You may be right." She gazed into his face. "We do have fun, don't we, Jack?"

"Yes, ma'am, we do."

She enjoyed looking into the blue of his eyes a moment longer. "We'd better get my purse," she said at last. "I left it lying on the grass."

"Ready to go back to the hotel?"

"There's one more office on our list, and it's just down the street."

"After all we've heard, I don't expect a different answer this time."

"Neither do I, but I won't be satisfied until I've explored every possibility."

He sighed. "Then let's go."

The office was smaller than many of the others they'd visited during the day, but neat. None of the plants had straggly, dead leaves and the couch in the front of the office blended well with the carpet. The place was deserted except for a woman with short blond hair who sat at the first of a row of four desks.

As Jack and Amy approached her, she glanced up from her paperwork and smiled. "May I help you?"

In spite of her fatigue, Amy smiled back. The woman had an open, friendly face. "We need to talk with one of your agents, but it looks as if they're all out of the office."

"Yes, they are, but perhaps I can be of some assistance. Won't you sit down?" She gestured to the pair of upholstered chairs facing her desk.

"Thanks, but if the agents are gone, we may as well not. You see, we need someone who can make a decision about listing some property for me. And we need the decision today."

The woman's gray eyes twinkled. "I think I could handle that. I'm the broker."

"Oh!" Amy grimaced. "What a sexist mistake. Just because you were a woman sitting at the front desk, I assumed—"

"It's okay." The woman chuckled. "I admit to doing this on purpose sometimes, just to throw people off. This isn't even my desk, but when no one else is in the office I like to move up here so I can watch the people walking by. I love being so close to Waikiki and all the action." She stood up and held out her hand. "I'm Rhonda Dandridge."

"Glad to meet you. I'm Amy Hobson and this is Jack Blickensderfer."

"Why don't you sit down and tell me about this listing you need such a quick decision on? Are you from the mainland?"

"Yes, and we're flying back tomorrow morning. A year ago I bought a lot, sight unseen, from a development company near Hana."

The blond woman nodded. "I know that development. It's been a little slow getting started, but it'll go eventually."

"I can't wait for eventually, Rhonda. I need to sell that lot now."

"Trouble with the payments?"

"No. But after visiting the site, I realize it doesn't fit my needs, or I should say my parents' needs. I want to sell that lot and find something else, probably here in Honolulu that's 'close to the action,' as you said."

Rhonda picked up a pencil with her left hand and began doodling on a pad of paper. "There are several unsold lots in that development. Reselling yours would be tough."

Amy glanced at Jack and braced herself for the same refusal she'd gotten all day. "But surely not impossible?"

The woman drew an arrow on the pad of paper. "Nothing's impossible." She looked at Amy. "But selling your lot would be close to it. What's on the plus side?"

Amy was taken aback. No one so far today had bothered to ask her what was good about the lot. How could she make it sound attractive to this woman? She thought quickly. "The view is terrific, and the lot is on the end of a street, next to the beach."

"Which is black sand. Not everyone goes for that."

"But they might, if it was advertised correctly. Black sand is exotic and different. Living near it could be made into a status symbol."

Rhonda stopped doodling and looked attentively at Amy. "Then there's that horrendous road. Perhaps someday it will be improved, but in the meantime—"

"In the meantime people have a secluded hideaway, living near the rich and famous. Don't several Hollywood stars have homes in the area?"

"Yes, but—"

"Then that should be mentioned as a selling point!" Amy warmed to her subject. She could tell Rhonda was considering the listing more seriously than anyone else had all day. "Another thing is all the fruit growing around there. I saw bananas, and I bet you could grow mangoes and papayas and who knows what else."

Rhonda smiled. "I think the development company should hire you to promote for them."

"No, thanks." Amy laughed. "I just want to find someone to sell my lot. If you can do that, then I'd like you to locate something else more suitable for my parents."

"You'd trust me to do that after your recent experience?"

"I have no choice. I can't afford to fly back here anytime soon. Besides, I have a better idea of what's here and what would be good for my parents. And yes, I think I do trust you. Will you list the lot for me?"

"Have you got any more real estate offices to consider?"

"No. You're the last."

"Then I'd like you to give me until early tomorrow morning to make my decision. When does your plane leave?"

"Eleven."

"Then we have time."

Amy felt a crazy mixture of hope and regret as she nodded her assent. She couldn't look at Jack. Intuition told her the woman would agree to list her lot and would probably sell it, too. The path toward her parents' dream was opening up again, even as the path leading to Jack grew dimmer. Amy could think of no way she could have everything she wanted. No way at all.

9

AMY AND JACK walked back to their rented Toyota in silence. Earlier in the day they'd decided to keep it and have their own transportation out to the airport the next morning. Finally, as they turned the car over to valet parking at the hotel and walked into the lobby, Jack spoke.

"I think you've found your gal."

"I think so, too."

Jack sighed. "We just had to visit one more real estate office, didn't we?"

"Yes, Jack, I'm afraid we did." His disappointment hurt her, but she had to remain strong in the face of it. "And checking every last possibility was the only way I could deal with the situation. I hope you understand that."

"I'm working on it."

She cringed at the despair in his voice. "My parents deserve this chance, Jack."

"And maybe they'll get it, after all. You gave a terrific sales pitch for your property, Amy."

"Rhonda drew those comments out of me when she asked about the plus side of the land. Dreaming up some good answers was an interesting challenge."

"With all the sales ideas you gave her, she'll probably move that lot in a week."

"Which is good," Amy said with as much enthusiasm as she could muster.

"I guess it is." He paused at the elevator. "Are you hungry? Maybe before we go up we should grab a bite to eat somewhere. There's a Japanese restaurant down the block, if you—"

Amy shook her head, silencing the rest of his suggestion. "No matter what happens tomorrow," she said softly, laying her hand on his forearm and gazing into eyes dulled with sadness, "we still have tonight. Do you want to spend the evening in a Japanese restaurant?"

"Is that a trick question?"

"Sort of, I guess. I'm trying to find out, in my own clumsy way, where we stand. Would you rather pretend last night never happened, or would you like to make the most of the last few hours we have together in Hawaii?"

"I'm not sure." He folded his arms and leaned against the wall next to the elevator while he studied her for several long seconds. Gradually his expression softened. His gaze grew warm and the straight line of his mouth curved into a tender smile. "As for pretending last night never happened, that's humanly impossible for me. As for the dinner suggestion—" He put his hands in his pockets and stared at the ceiling. "Room service sounds good. I seem to have lost my, uh, yen for Japanese food."

"Jack, that's a terrible pun." Amy grinned happily.

"And who knows?" He pushed away from the wall and punched the button to summon the elevator. "Maybe our broker lady won't want to list your property, after all."

"I have to hope she does."

Jack caught her chin between his thumb and forefinger and kissed her swiftly. "But I don't."

Once they were inside the room, Amy suggested Jack make himself comfortable on the bed while she, as she put it, "freshened up."

"You look pretty fresh to me, lady," he said, pinching her bottom.

"I'll tell you who's fresh around here," she retorted. "Now be a good boy and do as I say. You can order up a pitcher of mai-tais, if you like."

"You know what I'd like, and a fat, cold pitcher of mai-tais isn't even close. What I want is slim and—"

"Be quiet, Jack." She picked up the receiver and handed it to him. "Place the order and I'll be back in a jiffy."

"What a bossy lady. You'd better be making a legitimate trip in there," Jack grumbled, peering at the listings on the phone dial in order to find the number for room service.

While he was occupied Amy reached in the closet and pulled out the sarong that she hadn't worn the night before. This morning as Jack was taking a shower she'd made a secret vow to dazzle him tonight. Now was her chance.

With the bathroom door shut and locked so that Jack couldn't stroll in and spoil her surprise, she stripped off her clothes. A quick shower and a splash of cologne followed. Then she reached for her outfit for the evening.

Unhooking the silky length of pink-and-white material from its hanger, she held it in front of her. All day long Amy had observed the various ways Honolulu women wore the sarong, and she had made her choice.

Winding the colorful rectangle around her body by herself was tricky, but she managed the feat at last and tied the ends of the sarong above her breasts. Finally she surveyed herself in the bathroom mirror.

The effect was of a strapless gown that flowed gracefully over the thrust of her breasts down to the bright pink of her polished toenails. She looked regal enough to attend a black-tie dinner, yet underneath the sarong she was completely naked. One tug at the knot would reveal that fact, but she was reserving that privilege for only one man.

She brushed her long dark hair until it lay in a shining cascade over her shoulders. Her lei was nearly all wilted, but she found one orchid that had lasted and pulled it from the necklace to tuck behind her ear. She was ready.

Amy had no illusions of what the future held for her. Tied by the dependency of her parents and the debt she owed them, she couldn't afford the luxury of pursuing or being pursued by a man like Jack. And after what they'd shared, she'd miss him for the rest of her life. But one more night in his arms would fill her storehouse of memories for the lonely times ahead. Taking a deep breath, she opened the bathroom door.

Jack had followed her instructions by taking off his shoes and propping himself against the headboard. He was pouring them each a mai-tai from the tray beside the bed when she entered the room.

"I've got your drink here, if you—" He glanced in her direction as he was pouring and then did a double take.

"Jack, you're missing the glass completely," she said, trying not to laugh as he kept pouring the mai-tai mix directly onto the tray.

"Oh, yeah." He plunked the pitcher down and whirled back to her. "But who gives a damn about a little spilled rum at a time like this?"

"I thought you'd enjoy a nice surprise. I didn't know you'd flood the area with mai-tais," she chided.

"It's a fantastic surprise. Would you believe I'd forgotten all about that thing? Do you have on anything—" He swallowed. "Anything—"

Slowly she shook her head.

"This must be the spontaneity you talked about."

"The what?"

"You said once that cold weather robs you of spontaneity." He took a ragged breath. "I see what you mean."

"I hope so." Amy added a deliberately seductive sway to her walk as she crossed to the bed and sat beside him. Almost carelessly brushing her lips against his, she unbuttoned his shirt and slid both hands inside. "My goodness, but you're breathing hard," she murmured, tracing a path with her tongue down the corded muscles of his neck.

"It's tough work, serving up those mai-tais."

"Poor baby. You need to relax." Gradually she worked the shirt away from his broad shoulders and pulled it off each arm.

"Tell me," he said hoarsely. "What would happen if I untied this?" He reached for the knot above her breasts.

"Don't touch," Amy ordered, gently removing his hand from the material. "You're very impatient, Jack." She flicked her tongue against one puckered nipple. "On the islands we prefer a more leisurely pace." Her tongue left a moist trail across his chest as she nibbled her way to the second hard button secreted in a swirl of dark hair.

He groaned and licked dry lips. "It's been a long day, Amy. Have you no sympathy for a starving man?"

"None." She unhooked the fastening of his beltless slacks and slowly drew the zipper down.

Almost in unison with the zipper's rasp came his moan of pent-up desire. "Amy, this is torture."

"And you love it." She brushed her knuckles over the white briefs that restrained his bulging manhood and glanced into his hooded eyes. "Don't you?"

"Yes," he admitted with a rasp in his voice. "Even if I end up in a straitjacket."

"Oh, no. We can't let that happen. A straitjacket would cover far too much of this gorgeous body." She continued to stroke him. "How does that concept go— 'less is more'?"

"Something . . . like that."

"I believe in that concept, don't you?" The cotton material was warm and damp beneath her fingers.

"Sure do."

"Let's find out if it's true." Sliding both hands beneath the elastic of his briefs, she eased them off, taking the slacks at the same time. Tossing the clothes to the floor, she turned to gaze at his unfettered maleness. "Concept proven," she said softly.

"Come here." His fingers closed over her wrist, but she pulled away.

"Not yet, Jack." She placed a kiss on the inside of his thigh close to his knee and then a second one a little higher.

Jack shuddered as her lips made slow but certain progress toward their goal. "I hope you know what you're doing," he said with a gasp.

"We'll soon find out, won't we?"

"That isn't what I— My God, Amy... I don't know if I can— Where did you ever learn ..." He closed his eyes and moaned with pleasure. "Oh, lady. You... know what you're ... doing."

As she loved him, Amy felt passion building in her own body until she quivered with unsatisfied desire. Finally, unable to bear the tension, she kissed her way up the flat plane of his stomach and over the rounded contours of his chest, all the while rubbing her sarong-clad body over his heated skin.

"Untie me now, Jack," she whispered against his neck.

Fingers clumsy with desire, Jack fumbled with the knot and finally worked it free. The sarong loosened over her breasts and he pushed it down to bury his face against her creamy flesh.

"I will never get enough of you," he muttered, capturing a pouting nipple in his teeth.

Through the maelstrom of emotions buffeting her, Amy heard his words and wondered for a fleeting moment if this was the last time they'd ever be together like this. So much wanting, so much caring, and yet ...

Then she thought no more as he wrenched the sarong away and rolled her to lie on the silken fabric. The orchid tumbled from her hair and he picked it up, brushing the delicate petals over her breasts and down across the dark triangle covering her femininity to the softness of her inner thighs.

Then he made the same journey with the moist pressure of his lips and tongue. Carefully he sought out every nerve ending until she was overwhelmed by his fervent loving, enflamed by his passion. For a brief moment he left her and then he was back, parting her thighs with a demanding knee, seeking the union they could delay no longer.

Joyously they celebrated their pleasure with murmurs of praise and cries of delight. Their skin glistened in the dim light as the setting sun filtered in through the lanai doors. From a distance the drums of a luau beat a primitive rhythm as the two bodies twisted on the bright fabric of the sarong.

Their movements became more urgent as desire gripped them and wrung moans of passion from their lips. The force grew greater and greater, until at last the fist opened and hurled them over the abyss into a chasm of total sensation that left them gasping for breath.

"Amy," Jack whispered as he collapsed against her.

"I'm here," she choked out. "I'm here, my darling."

Much later, as she lay in the darkness listening to his even breathing, she wondered how much longer she would be there for him.

THE TELEPHONE woke them the next morning. Jack picked up the receiver, mumbled something Amy couldn't hear and passed it over to her, stretching the cord across his bare chest.

Amy scrambled to a sitting position and placed her hand over the mouthpiece. "Who is it?" she asked Jack softly.

"Real estate lady," Jack whispered back.

Amy glanced past him to the clock on the bedside table. Apparently this woman's business day started at seven. If she sold property with this much energy, she'd have the lot unloaded in no time, Amy decided.

Amy cleared her throat and uncovered the mouthpiece. "Hello?"

"Sorry if I woke you up, but I didn't want to miss you this morning."

"That's okay, Ms. Dandridge." Amy reached down and stilled the masculine hand that was creeping up her thigh.

"Rhonda. Call me Rhonda. Anyway, I've been thinking very carefully about your property, and about you."

"Me?" Amy frowned sternly at Jack as he began to tickle the inside of her thigh once more.

"Yes. What sort of job do you have on the mainland?"

"I'm a secretary for a lumber...company." Amy crossed her legs and glared at Jack, who only grinned in response and pantomimed biting the phone cord in two.

"A secretary? That's ridiculous."

"I beg your pardon?" Amy tried to ignore Jack. The conversation was confusing enough without his distractions.

"You should be in sales, Amy," Rhonda continued. "It's written all over you. I have an excellent eye for good salespeople, and you'd be wonderful."

"That's nice of you to say, but what has that got to do with listing my property?" Amy turned away from Jack, but he used the opportunity to put tiny kisses along the curve of her spine.

"I'm willing to list it, but I have a condition."

"What's that?" Amy reached behind her, grabbed Jack's earlobe and pinched hard. With a muffled yowl he rolled away from her in mock agony.

On the other end of the line, Rhonda took a deep breath. "My condition is that you agree to work for me."

"Work for you?" Amy turned to stare in bewilderment at Jack. "I don't understand."

"I need another agent in the office. I'd pay for your training and licensing in exchange for an agreement that you'd stay in Honolulu for a minimum of two years. You can oversee the sale of your land and find something more suitable yourself, probably in a shorter time. And if my instincts are correct about your sales abilities, you'll have more money to work with."

"I'm...I'm stunned, Rhonda. I never expected this." Amy noticed that all the playfulness was gone from Jack's expression. He was regarding her silently, watchfully.

"Will you do it? I don't think you'll be sorry."

"There are lots of considerations, Rhonda. My parents depend on me a great deal. I'd be so far away." Amy saw Jack's eyes narrow and knew he was guessing the trend of the conversation.

"That's right, you did say this land was for your parents, not yourself."

"Yes. I'm buying it for them."

"Were you planning to move over here, too, then?"

"Well, yes, I was."

"Perfect! If they can manage without you for a few short months, you'll be able to sell the land you don't want, buy what you think they'd like better and move them right over. You'll already be established in a career. I assume you'd planned to work when you got here."

"I did, but—"

"And your parents must not need daily attention or you couldn't have made this trip."

"True, but I'm really not sure about this."

"Of course you're not. When people move ahead in life, they have to take steps they're not sure about."

"I have so many thoughts running through my head right now."

"Do any of them have to do with the fellow who answered the phone?"

"I, uh—"

"That's okay. I'm sure he's listening to every word, and I'm also sure he's a factor in your decision. I'm all in favor of love, Amy, but not at the expense of your whole future. And you do have a future here. I can feel it."

"We aren't . . . that is, I'm not in—" Amy stopped abruptly before uttering the same word Rhonda had used to describe the relationship between Jack and Amy.

"Oh, you two are in love, all right. What are the chances you could talk him into moving here with you?"

"Not good." Amy was afraid to meet Jack's penetrating gaze. Love? Well, of course she'd always loved Jack in a sisterly sort of way. But love with a capital letter, the kind that led to white lace and promises? Amy remembered Jack's reference to beans in a jar, and a tingling started in the soles of her feet and worked its way upward. What kind of choice was she being asked to make?

"I wouldn't be too sure you couldn't talk him into it, Amy. I saw the way he looked at you yesterday. How about giving it a shot? And even if he won't go along with the idea, please give this serious consideration and call me back before you leave."

"And you won't list the property unless I agree?"

"Oh, I probably would, but I really am shorthanded right now. You saw three empty desks and I only have two agents to fill them. I honestly won't have as much time and personnel to spend unless you take my offer."

"But why me? I imagine you have lots of people looking for a job in Honolulu."

"That's true, but damned few have what it takes to make it in real estate, and then there's the matter of island fever."

"What?" Amy clutched the phone. "You mean a disease?"

Rhonda laughed. "Sort of. Ever hear of cabin fever? This is the same thing, except that people begin to feel claustrophobic about being on an island in the middle of a very big ocean."

"Oh."

"Not everyone gets it, but that's why I made the stipulation that you'd have to sign on for two years. I don't want to waste my investment in you."

"Rhonda, can I call you back in an hour or so with my answer?"

"Sure thing. Talk it over with that boyfriend of yours. And keep your options open, Amy."

"I'll . . . I'll try. Goodbye." Amy handed the receiver to Jack.

He replaced it in the cradle and leaned back against the headboard with his arms folded. "Well?"

"She's offering me a job selling real estate."

"I pretty much gathered that."

Amy twisted the end of the sheet into a bulky rope. She should be happy, and instead she felt like a condemned person at the gallows. "For some reason she thinks I'd be good at it."

"You probably would." His face was expressionless.

"I don't know if Mom and Dad could manage without me, though, even for a few months, like she said," Amy ventured.

Jack gazed at a painting of tropical birds hanging on the opposite wall. "I think they could manage, Amy. Especially if you asked Brad to check on them every so often. He could fly over a couple of times. In between, I'd be glad to—"

Amy clenched the sheet in her fist. "Stop it, Jack."

"Stop what?" He looked at her with a steady gaze.

"Stop sounding so nonchalant about this, as if—" Her voice broke for a moment and she worked to regain control. "As if you don't care if I accept the offer or not."

His speech was slow and deliberate. "Of course I care, Amy. But this woman is giving you a golden opportunity to get what you want for your parents. Isn't that why we're here in the first place?"

"Yes, but—"

"I don't see how you can turn down this chance, Amy."

Hot tears stung her eyes. "You're not going to try and talk me out of coming over here? She's asking for a commitment of two years, Jack."

"If everything works out, you'll be here a lot longer than two years."

"And what about us?"

Jack looked at her and shrugged.

"That's it? You're giving up just like that?"

"I don't have much choice."

"You most certainly do." She was rigid with apprehension, but she had to ask, had to know. "You could consider moving to Hawaii, for one thing."

The answer was in his eyes even before he shook his head. "No, Amy, I'm afraid I couldn't."

10

AMY'S PRIDE warned her to leave his answer at that, but what they'd shared in the past two days and nights overrode her pride. "Why not?" she asked, and hated the way her voice quavered. Jack appeared unperturbed by the turn of events, while she was dying inside. Was he made of stone?

Jack uncrossed his arms and got out of bed. "Because moving to Hawaii is your dream, not mine. I'm going to take a shower."

"Wait a minute, Jack." Amy hurried after him into the bathroom. "Hawaii is really my parents' dream. Can I help it if they need me around to make their dream come true? You can't blame me for that."

He turned on the water and adjusted the temperature without looking at her. "It's not a question of blame. You've just stated the facts as you see them. There's no room for me in that scenario."

"If you cared enough there would be."

Steam from the shower billowed out around the tan plastic curtain as Jack stood very still with his back to her. Finally he turned around. "Cared enough for what? To leave a job I'm happy with and a part of the country I'm fond of? To desert the illiteracy program I've given months of effort, just when the crucial period of designing and building the reading center has arrived?"

Amy couldn't respond. She was asking a lot, but what about the passion between them? The rush of the water was the only sound in the room as they stared at each other.

At last Jack rubbed the back of his neck and looked away. "I'm not denying that the past two days have been special, Amy. But they're not enough to tear up my whole life over. Especially when I imagine moving here, making all the sacrifices, only to discover that your half-baked schemes aren't working out."

"Half-baked schemes? Is that what you think of my plans?"

"I wouldn't say you're on solid ground, would you? You have some land which may or may not sell and a job offer which may or may not materialize into something you want to make a career of. You might find another retirement spot for your parents and you might not. What if you're ready to go home in six months, Amy? Where does that leave me?"

Amy clenched her jaw. "I see. Brad's little sister is up to another of her crazy stunts, right?"

"Amy, you've got boundless energy and lots of spunk. If you ever harness that productively, you'll go far. Maybe this real estate thing will be your answer. But I'm not ready to give up everything I've worked for on the off chance that it will be. Not when Hawaii isn't my choice of places to live, anyway."

"Well, heaven forbid that you'd go out on a limb for me, Jack." Amy's eyes narrowed in rage. "But I'll tell you something. I'm going to make it in this new job. I'm going to sell that land and find a better deal for my parents. Brad's little sister is not going to screw this up."

He looked at her for a long moment. "I think you'd better make your call."

"Yes, I'd better." She turned and stalked out of the bathroom.

RHONDA GAVE AMY three weeks to settle her affairs in Bellingham. Handing in her notice at work was easy; confronting her parents was not. She'd called them the day she'd returned from Hawaii, but talking to them on the telephone didn't seem to be the right way to broach the subject, so she'd babbled on about how wonderful the weather had been and had promised to come over sometime during the weekend.

Rather than make a big announcement to both of them, Amy decided to tell each one separately, starting with her mother. On Saturday afternoon she drove to her parents' neat, white clapboard house. She went in the back door, hoping to catch her mother first. She was in luck. Her mother was in the laundry room, folding clothes.

"Amy!" The tiny woman dropped the towel she was folding and hurried over to hug her daughter. "How's the world traveler?"

"Still suffering from jet lag, I think." Amy's eyes misted for a moment as she returned the hug. She breathed in the familiar scent of laundry soap and clothes warm from the dryer. For so long she'd taken this familiar environment for granted, but in a little more than two weeks she'd be an ocean away from this house. She'd never counted on being homesick, but she certainly felt homesick right then.

"Didn't Jack come with you?"

"No." Amy turned to the pile of laundry and began folding. "We, uh, had a slight disagreement." She'd tried hard not to think of Jack at all since he had dropped her off at her apartment last Tuesday. Whenever his program came on the radio, she changed to another station.

"Amy, I'm sorry." Her mother touched her arm. "I thought something special was happening between you two, and I was so happy about it. Jack is almost like a member of this family. He's so much like Brad."

True, Amy thought bitterly. *He and Brad both think I'm crazy.* "Well, it didn't work out, Mom," she said aloud, adding another towel to the growing pile.

"Don't give up on him yet. You're both young and you have time." Her mother winked. "Who knows?"

"We may be young, but we don't exactly have time."

"What do you mean?"

"I—" Amy glanced at her mother and looked away again. "I have a job offer in Hawaii. I'm going to take it."

"A job in Hawaii?" Amy's mother clutched a floral-print pillowcase to her breast. "What kind of job?"

"Selling real estate."

"But Amy, you've never—"

"I know, Mom. The broker, who's a woman, has agreed to send me to school. This is a wonderful chance."

"I guess so." Her mother stared in bewilderment at the pile of clothes. Then she began sorting through it, as if looking for something, yet picking up nothing. "You'd leave Bellingham and go all the way over there, for . . . for good?"

"We can keep in touch by phone, Mom." Amy put an arm around her narrow shoulders. "And Brad will check on things."

"He only comes home once a year, Amy."

"Then he can make it more often. Spokane's not that far away. Besides, I'll be home to visit in less than six months. I promise."

"I hear it's very expensive to live there. How can you start a new job and afford to fly home in six months? I wonder if that real estate woman has led you on, Amy."

A lump of self-pity rose in Amy's throat. Even her mother believed that she was too gullible for her own good. "That's not logical, Mom. Rhonda's paying for my ticket back and enrolling me in real estate classes. Why would she put out money on my behalf if she didn't think I'd do well?"

"You're right, I suppose. But Amy, you'll be so far away...."

"It'll be okay, Mom." The apprehension on her mother's face almost pulled the rest of the story out of Amy, but she restrained herself. Although she believed she'd be able to move her parents to Hawaii in less than six months, she couldn't promise anyone that she would, least of all this vulnerable little woman.

Her mother smoothed a pillowcase with one small hand. "I hope so. Have you told your father?"

"No."

"He's in the living room watching golf. You'd better go tell him."

Amy nodded. She wasn't looking forward to his reaction.

As she entered the living room, he glanced up from the screen. "Hi, there. Did you bring any pictures of the trip?"

Amy was taken aback. She hadn't even thought of taking pictures, and yet any normal person would have shot rolls of film. "No, Dad. I forgot my camera."

He shook his head. "Figures. I swear, Amy Hobson, you are the most scatterbrained female."

"Dad, I need to talk to you about something. Could we turn off the TV for a little while?"

Her father picked up the remote control and reduced the volume. "No need to turn it all the way off. Say, this is some set that Brad got us last Christmas."

"Dad, he bought you that set two years ago."

"He did? Nah, I don't think so, Amy. Anyway, it's a small detail." He waved one hand in the air as he watched Ben Crenshaw sink a difficult putt. "That guy can really play the game."

Amy sensed an opening and grabbed it. "You know, Dad, I think you spend too much time worrying about small details. Mom could do some of the worrying around here, like when the bills are due and things like that."

He glanced away from the screen and his eyes narrowed. "I've always paid the bills, and I'll continue to do it. I bring in the money, don't I?"

"That's the point. Why do everything?"

"I don't. Your mother is responsible for the house and the meals, and I'm responsible for bringing in the money and paying it out. We've got a good system." His attention returned to the television screen.

Amy sighed. Should she confront him with the times she'd had to bargain with the electric company because of an overdue bill her father had forgotten to pay? Should she mention that he'd driven without car insurance for an entire six months because renewing the policy slipped his mind? She couldn't say those things.

Amy looked up as her mother came into the room.

"Well, Virgil, what do you think of Amy's new job plans?"

"Mom, I haven't—"

"What new job plans?" her father said sharply. "She hasn't told me about any new job."

"Oh." Her mother twisted her hands together. "I thought by now she'd have mentioned it."

"I was just about to tell—"

"She's moving to Hawaii," her mother said quickly. "Isn't that wonderful, Virgil?"

"The hell she is!" Her father slapped the arm of his leather recliner. "Amy alone in Hawaii? That's a laugh."

Amy clenched her fists. He knew so well how to hurt her. "Then I guess you'll have all the chuckles you need for a while, Dad. I'm going."

"To do what?"

She considered leaving the room. He'd only ridicule her plans. But a pleading glance from her mother kept Amy from moving. The two women had discussed how the accident had made Virgil more caustic than ever, and Amy's mother had often begged her daughter's understanding.

Amy took a calming breath. "When Jack and I were over there we met—"

"Are you going with Jack? That's different."

"No, I am not going with Jack. A real estate broker in Honolulu has offered me a job. I'm leaving in less than three weeks."

"And the real estate lady is sending Amy to school, Virgil."

Her father regarded them with a baleful expression. "Fine thing. Amy goes off to Hawaii and we can't because her lousy boyfriend cheated us out of—"

"Virgil! You promised we'd never throw that up to her. It wasn't Amy's fault."

Amy looked directly at her father. "Yes, it was. I brought Philip over here. You invested in his program because I vouched for him."

"And I should have known better."

Amy bit her lip. "I'll make it up to you someday, Dad. I promise."

"How?" Apprehension tinged his voice. "By running off to Hawaii yourself and leaving us here alone?"

For a brief moment Amy glimpsed the vulnerability he tried so hard to hide, and her attitude softened. "I'll be back for a visit soon, and maybe . . . maybe someday we can all live over there." It was more than she'd intended to say, but she couldn't help tossing out some sort of hope to them.

Her father focused on the television again. "I wouldn't count on it."

Her mother touched Amy's arm. "Come on and help me start supper," she said gently.

With one last glance at her father, Amy started from the room.

"Amy?"

She turned at the sound of his voice, but he still appeared to be intent on the golf match. "Did you say something, Dad?"

"Yes. I want you to remember that if you get stuck over there with no money to come home, I'll send you whatever you need."

She didn't know whether to be furious or not. He cared for her, but he didn't believe in her. That seemed to be the pattern for the men in her life these days. "Thanks, Dad," she said at last.

The next day when Amy called Brad, she told him only that she was accepting a job in Honolulu, but nothing of her plans for their parents. Brad's response was only slightly less acerbic than her father's had been.

"None of you have faith in me!" Amy complained bitterly into the receiver. "Not you, or Mom and Dad, or Jack."

"Face it, Amy. We all love you very much, but we've bailed you out of a million scrapes. This looks like another one about to happen. I think you should stay home, cultivate whatever's happening between you and Jack and forget moving to Hawaii. You've been listening to Dad's stories about the place too much. Hell, if real estate is your new interest, check into the situation around Bellingham."

"I prefer Hawaii, Brad."

"Don't we all? But that's an expensive place to live, Amy, and you're so far away from everything and everybody."

"Brad, are you upset because I won't be here to watch over Mom and Dad?"

"Nope. I never have approved of you tying yourself to them. I've told you that before."

"Somebody has to do it, and I'm counting on you to take over, Brad."

"And I will, within reason. But if Dad screws something up, and Mom doesn't have you to call, maybe she'll realize she has to fend for herself once in a while."

"I'm not sure she can."

"Maybe we'll find out, baby sister."

"I wish you wouldn't call me that."

"Sorry. It slipped out."

"Brad, promise you'll call them once a week and check on things. A visit in the next two or three months wouldn't hurt, either."

"I'll do the best I can, but you're the one I'm worried about, not them. If you get into any trouble over there, call me collect, okay?"

Amy sighed. Brad was repeating her father's reaction almost exactly. "Okay. But I don't plan to have any news that can't be put in a letter. Goodbye, Brad."

"So long and good luck, ba—uh, I mean, sis."

Amy hung up the telephone. Everyone had been notified except Steve, who was coming over Wednesday night to negotiate a new contract. She'd have to tell him there would be no more contracts. On the plane ride home Jack had offered to take over Steve's reading lessons, and Amy had accepted. Steve should be pleased, considering how much he admired the disk jockey.

Jack. Her body ached every time her mind whispered his name. She had hoped that once they left the place where they had shared such passion she would forget about the hours they'd lain naked in each other's arms. Bellingham held no such memories, nor did her apartment. So why was she haunted by him?

She'd wake up in the middle of the night because she imagined him lying next to her. Or standing in front of her bathroom mirror applying makeup, she'd think he spoke, and she'd have to walk through the entire apartment to convince herself no one was there.

She longed for the caressing sound of his wonderful voice, even if she couldn't have him physically with her. Giving in to the urge she'd been ignoring for several days, Amy turned on one of her radios and adjusted the dial to Jack's station. Only after another deejay announced the next song did she remember that Jack didn't work on Sunday nights.

STEVE SURPRISED AMY on Wednesday night by arriving with their contract already drawn up. He was so proud of having written the document himself that Amy hated to dampen his enthusiasm with her announcement that she couldn't sign it. But she had no choice.

"Steve, there's been a major change in my life," she began hesitantly.

He grinned. "You and Jack, huh? Hey, if you two are planning a honeymoon or something, I can fix this contract to make time for that."

"Well, no, that's not it. I'm moving to Hawaii. I have a job offer there."

"Moving?" His unruly thatch of hair still covered any expression in his eyes, but his mouth turned down in disappointment. "Then I guess you won't need this." He folded up the contract into a small square and stuffed it in his pants pocket.

"Jack will," Amy said hastily. "The tutoring won't stop, just because I'm leaving. You're doing so well, Steve. You can continue with Jack, and you'll hardly know I'm gone."

"Bull." He glanced up quickly and flushed. "Sorry," he mumbled and looked away again.

"Steve, I'm really touched. I didn't know these sessions meant so much to you."

He shuffled his feet. "Yeah, well, I sorta got used to them, I guess. Sorta got used to having you teach me. I mean, Jack's okay, but . . ."

"Thank you, Steve," Amy said softly. "And I wish with all my heart that this job didn't mean we have to give up our Wednesday-night sessions. But this is a chance in a lifetime, and I have to take it."

Steve tilted his head back and looked at her from under his hair. "If Jack's teaching me reading, then he's not going to Hawaii with you, is he?"

"No."

He regarded her with the wise understanding and sympathy of a sixteen-year-old who has also loved and lost. "You two split, huh?"

"Yes."

"Kinda tough, I bet."

"Yes." Amy's throat constricted. She mustn't cry in front of this boy. "But it's for the best."

Steve nodded. "Hope so."

So do I, Amy thought fervently as she forced a smile to her lips for the cheerful goodbye she was determined to exchange with Steve. When he was gone, she went into the kitchen and packed and cleaned until she was exhausted.

Her parents had agreed to store anything she wasn't taking to Hawaii, and she made several trips to their house during the days before she was scheduled to leave. Both her mother and father tried to joke about her strange assortment of possessions, especially the

Cheez Whiz, but Amy could tell they were agitated about her impending departure.

She ate dinner with them the last night she was to be in town. The conversation at the table was disjointed, both because of her father's lapses of memory and Amy's own preoccupation with the details of moving. Mentally she ticked off the final arrangements.

She'd sleep in her apartment tonight and turn over the key to her landlord in the morning. After much debate about what to do with her car, Amy had decided to drive it to Seattle and have it shipped over to Honolulu. Her suitcases were by the front door of the apartment; her outfit for the trip was hanging in the now-empty closet.

At nine o'clock she hugged her parents quickly and left to avoid having her mother's tears touch off a cascade of her own. The March night was rainy and cold, which should have made her more delighted with her decision to leave Bellingham, perhaps permanently.

Then why did the town suddenly seem more appealing than ever? She drove past her high school, and her favorite stores. She cruised past the lumberyard and drove down by the bay to watch the lights of small boats bobbing gently. Parking by the water, she shut off the engine and listened to the soft patter of the rain on the roof of the car.

Tonight she was on the edge of the mainland, looking west toward Hawaii. Tomorrow night she'd be gazing back from a shore hundreds of miles away. None of it seemed real to her. At last, unable to stop herself, she switched the ignition to battery power and turned on her car radio to KPLY.

The upbeat song by Phil Collins didn't match her melancholy mood, but Amy wasn't listening for the sake of the music. She needed to hear Jack's voice once more before she left. Impatiently she waited for the song to end. All she wanted was a few seconds of that magic voice, and she'd turn off the radio and go home to bed. Just a few seconds.

Instead a commercial followed the song, and Amy drummed her fingers on the dashboard. What had begun as an impulse had become a critical requirement for her. What if his schedule had been changed and he was off duty tonight? Or he might be sick. No, Jack wasn't ever sick.

"It's nine forty-six here at KPLY."

His velvet voice ran through her like electric current and she gripped the steering wheel with both hands.

"And I wouldn't be surprised if it's nine forty-six where you are, unless you're one of those compulsive types who sets clocks three minutes ahead to make sure you're never late."

"Oh, Jack." Tears gathered in Amy's eyes, and she leaned her head against the steering wheel.

"Cousin Ernie's been late to his job the past few mornings. Did I tell you what he does? Freezes peas. You know, those plastic bags of peas that say 'individually frozen'? Ernie does that. Well, somebody has to."

Amy couldn't decide if she was laughing or crying.

"Hey, any of you crazies running around in this drizzle? Old Jack is heading straight home pretty soon for a warm armchair and a cold brewsky. So put that in your corncob and smoke it, Mom. I do so have sense enough to come in out of the rain. Unless it's purple. And speaking of 'Purple Rain,' here's Prince."

Amy hadn't let herself cry since returning to Bellingham, but the sound of Jack's voice after three long weeks without him swept away her self-control. Her sobs stayed cocooned inside the little white car; her gasping breath fogged up the windows. Alone. She was so alone.

"That about wraps it up for another night, ladies and gentlemen. See you tomorrow night at six. The news is coming up next, so pay attention. Keep informed. Keep the faith. And most of all, keep listening to the hottest radio station in all of Whatcom County, KPLY-FM."

Amy swiped at her wet cheeks. No more Jack. He was off the air and by tomorrow night, she'd be beyond the reach of the station's transmitters. Beyond Jack's reach.

She sat staring at the fogged windshield for several minutes. Then, with puppetlike movements, she turned on the engine and started the defroster. Then she sent the beam of her headlights into the rain-splashed darkness.

Amy knew she should go home. After putting the car in reverse, she backed out of the parking space. Mechanically she negotiated the slick streets toward her apartment, but at the last minute she swung the car left instead of right. She had to see him tonight, no matter what it cost both of them in the months ahead.

11

AMY CHECKED for his black Camaro in the parking space before ringing the doorbell. Although he'd told his listeners he was going straight home, she couldn't assume he had. Her heart pounded as she waited in the misty rain. She didn't even know if he'd be alone. Maybe she should have called first. But that would have been the logical thing to do, and Amy wasn't dealing in logic tonight.

At the sound of the doorbell Jack started from his melancholy reverie. For a brief moment he wondered if— But no, that was a crazy idea. If she hadn't contacted him in three weeks, why would she appear tonight, just before she was ready to leave?

He put down the can of beer that had chilled his fingers but was beginning to warm the cold place in his heart. Maybe it was Beeper or Steve. Both boys had an unusual life-style and either one could show up on his doorstep at any hour.

Heaving himself from the overstuffed chair, Jack walked to the door. He didn't feel like counseling somebody tonight. He had plenty of problems of his own, without listening to the woes of a teenager. He used to think he could relate to them, but tonight he felt like a bitter old man. Relating would be difficult.

He unlocked the door and opened it just the width of his body and braced himself to behave with some trace of compassion. When he saw her standing on his worn green welcome mat, he blinked and pressed his forefinger and thumb to the corners of his eyes.

When he looked again, she was still there, haloed in raindrops that glittered in the porch light like bits of Christmas tinsel. Her hands were stuffed in the pockets of her partially zipped windbreaker, and the dampness of the night had curled and tousled her dark hair in the way he remembered so well from their days in Hawaii. A raindrop splashed against her cheek. He reached to wipe it away and stopped. If she was a dream, his touch would make her disappear.

"Jack?"

His gaze went to her firm, pink lips. Once he'd kissed them until they were swollen with the force of his mouth against hers. "You're here," he said slowly. "Why?"

"I'm leaving tomorrow."

"I know. I didn't expect to see you again." He searched for answers behind the sadness and confusion reflected in her brown eyes.

Her smile was tremulous. "I was listening to you on the radio tonight, and I decided that I couldn't leave without . . ."

"Without what, Amy?"

"Never mind. I made a mistake." She whirled and ran down the walk.

"No, wait!" He charged into the rain after her, his feet smashing through puddles. He caught her arm and spun her around. "Wait just a damned minute."

"I had no business coming here." She turned her head away. "I should have left everything the way it was."

The damp nylon of her windbreaker rustled as his fingers tightened on her arm. "But you couldn't." His shirt absorbed the steady drip of the rain.

"So I'm weak." Her voice quavered. "Let me disappear from your life, Jack. We'll only make this more difficult if we . . ."

"If we what?" He held her chin and forced her to look at him. Her eyelashes were spiky with the rain, and her lips glistened. He couldn't take his gaze from the temptation of that mouth that he knew so maddeningly well. "Why did you show up here tonight?"

"I don't know." Her eyes filled with tears.

"But I do." He pushed his fingers through her hair and held her still. "You're here for this." His lips came down hard against hers and he drove his tongue inside. She tried to twist away, but he held her fast and savored the heated interior of her sweet mouth. God, but he loved to kiss her.

She moaned and began to relax in his grip. He ran his hand up her arm and inside the collar of her jacket. She shuddered as he stroked her throat.

He lifted his mouth a fraction away from hers. "You came for some loving, didn't you, Amy?" he murmured.

"No," she insisted unsteadily. "I just wanted to see you once more."

"Tell the truth and shame the devil." His hand trailed to the ridge of her collarbone. "You wanted one more memory to take across the ocean."

"No, I—" She was breathing hard.

"Amy, you can't pretend with me anymore." He reached inside her windbreaker and stroked the taut nipple that pushed against the material of her blouse. "I know too much."

"But Jack, what kind of a woman would throw herself at a man the night before she leaves town?"

He cupped her breast and brushed his lips against hers. "Someone who doesn't have enough sense to come in out of the rain, maybe."

"You must think I'm a total idiot."

"How could I?" He kneaded the swell of her breast, although touching her was causing a painful bind against the buttons of his jeans. "I'm out here with you."

"So your mother was right," she said languidly.

"Apparently." He nuzzled her neck. "Ready to go in?"

"Jack, maybe it would be better if we didn't."

"I doubt that. Making love on a wet sidewalk doesn't appeal to me."

"I meant not make love at all."

"You don't want that and you know it."

"But what about tomorrow?"

"Don't think about tomorrow. Let's just love each other, Amy. I need you as much as you need me."

"Even if this is the end for us?"

"Especially if this is the end." He kissed her fiercely and led her inside.

After all they'd shared, Amy found it strange that she'd never seen his bedroom. But then he'd never seen hers, either. Their relationship had existed in a kind of vacuum, unrelated to their everyday existence.

She suspected he'd rented the apartment furnished, just as she had hers, so she couldn't read his taste in the walnut veneer of the headboard or the ginger jar lamp on the bedside table. Across from the double bed was a large dresser and an attached mirror where a bright pink Frisbee hung over one corner and a brown shriveled loop dangled limply from the other side.

She disentangled herself from Jack's possessive grip and walked over to the mirror. "You've still got the Frisbee."

"It reminds me of a good friend. We've shared a lot of laughs."

"And this other thing looks like—"

"It is."

"I thought you threw it away."

"I started to, but I ended up tucking it in a side pocket of my suitcase. Looks pretty miserable, I know."

"No, it doesn't." She fingered the dried remains of baby orchids, and sorrow constricted her throat. "I missed you, Jack."

He came up behind her and wrapped her in his arms. "I missed you, too," he said in a husky voice. His gaze met hers in the mirror. "I kept hoping you'd call."

"I thought staying away was best. I tried, Jack, but tonight, when I heard you on the radio . . ."

He buried his nose in her hair. "You smell like rain."

"You mean all soggy?"

"No." He turned her around and slowly unzipped her jacket. "Like a bed of petunias in the morning before the dew is gone. Like a deep, cool well on a hot day." He pushed the jacket over her arms and tossed it aside. "Like melting snow." He undid the first few buttons of her blouse.

"I love you, Jack."

He stopped unbuttoning and looked into her eyes.

"It's true," she whispered in an awed voice. "I shouldn't have said it now, but it's true. I love you."

He cupped her face in both hands. "No, you shouldn't have said it now. But you did. Oh, Amy!"

She gazed into the tortured blue of his eyes. "What are we going to do?"

"I can't speak for you, only for me."

She swallowed hard. "And?"

"I'm going to love the hell out of you." His eyes blazed with intensity. "When you're alone over there, I want you to remember everything that happens tonight in Technicolor detail. I want you to ache for me, Amy."

She shivered as he wrenched the last buttons loose and discarded her blouse on the floor with her windbreaker. In a few seconds he'd added her bra to the pile and drawn her toward him. His damp shirt was cool against her heated skin.

He gazed down at the swell of her breasts nestling against him. "You're so beautiful," he murmured, stroking her back. "I've dreamed of having you here, holding you like this, touching you again, like this, and this. . . ." He pushed back her hair and nibbled her earlobe before tracing the curve of her neck with his tongue.

Amy arched in his embrace, offering herself to his moist caress. When his mouth captured the tip of one breast, she closed her eyes with a moan of satisfaction. He was right. She had wanted this, just once more before giving him up forever, giving up the man she loved. He fumbled with the catch on her slacks and she helped him, as anxious to be out of her clothes as he was to take them off.

He looked at her and smiled. "Where's my sarong?"

"I wish I'd worn it," she murmured, stepping out of her shoes and then the slacks, which dropped with a swish to the floor.

His gaze moved to her white lace panties. "Take them off for me, Amy."

She slid the panties over her hips and watched his nostrils flare with desire. Then the panties joined the rest of her clothing on the floor.

"Just stand there a minute," he said softly. "Let me look at the woman I love."

Heat flashed through her and her voice quavered. "You shouldn't have said that, either."

"No, I had to say it." He gazed into her eyes. "I love you, Amy. I hadn't planned to tell you." He stepped forward and wove his fingers through her hair. "But if I have to let you go, knowing you love me, then I want you to understand how I feel—how much your leaving will hurt."

She snuggled against him and laid her cheek on his chest. "I'm sorry."

"Me too."

Her silent tears fell on his already damp shirt. She seemed to have a talent for hurting the ones she loved. In the process of correcting the damage done to her parents, she was making Jack miserable. And herself.

"Don't cry." He held her tight and kissed the top of her head.

"But I've made such a mess of things. As usual."

Jack stroked her hair. "We've made a mess of things together, Amy. I'm taking half the blame for this. If I'd steered clear of you from the beginning, we wouldn't have these problems." He tipped her tear-streaked face upward. "But I'm glad I didn't steer clear, Amy."

"Even after all that's happened?"

"You bet. I wouldn't have missed loving you for the world."

"Oh, Jack." She kissed him tenderly, but the gentle mingling of their lips soon became forceful and demanding. Her fingers flew down the buttons of his shirt, and she shoved the damp material aside to stroke his bare torso. "I need you, Jack," she murmured against his mouth.

He lifted his head and gazed down at her. "I've never wanted anyone like this," he confessed. "Can you feel me shaking?"

"I thought that was me." She rubbed the lower half of her body back and forth across the rough denim of his jeans. "Take these off, Jack," she coaxed, pressing against his swelling masculinity.

Jack groaned and pressed back. "My thoughts exactly."

"I'll turn down the covers." She slipped reluctantly from the warmth of his arms and walked across to the bed. After tossing back the spread and top sheet, she glanced over her shoulder and found him standing just as she'd left him, watching her.

"I love the way you move."

She stretched out on the cool sheets and smiled seductively. "I love the way you move, too. I only wish you'd move a little faster."

He shrugged out of his shirt and nudged off his shoes. "When I look at that luscious body, I forget what I'm supposed to be doing."

"Need a reminder?" She rolled languidly to her side.

"Not anymore."

Bracing her cheek on her palm, Amy feasted on the emerging glory of his body. "Now it's your turn to stand there for a minute," she said breathlessly. Carefully she memorized the swirl of his dark chest hair, the faint ripple of his ribs, the flat plane of his stomach. Her gaze moved downward to the chiseled beauty of hips and thighs, and the burgeoning evidence of his passion for her. Could she bear to leave him? She would have to. Somehow. Amy held out her hand to him, knowing it might be for the last time.

AMY LEFT while Jack was sleeping. She couldn't risk the pain of saying goodbye. If she didn't have to see his blue eyes darken in anguish, she could keep her memory of his loving gaze intact.

She kept a tight rein on her own emotions, pushing herself to finish packing and leave Bellingham before dawn. She put her apartment keys in an envelope and left them in the landlord's mailbox. Then she drove out of the morning-quiet town and tried not to think. She'd made her choice and she couldn't back out now.

When the plane landed in Honolulu, Amy was numb with exhaustion and loneliness. She wished Rhonda hadn't insisted on meeting her at the airport. Amy didn't feel fit for polite company. Besides, her suit was wrinkled and her makeup was in bad need of repair. Rhonda would probably take one look at her and decide that this new employee wouldn't work out at all.

But when Rhonda greeted her with a smile and a white lei to put around her neck, Amy hugged her new friend with gratitude. The tears she'd kept at bay threatened to spill out as the scent of the flowers brought memories of Jack, but Amy blinked them

away. All of Honolulu would probably remind her of
Jack. She couldn't let the memories bother her.

"I've found you the cutest apartment up near Diamond Head!" Rhonda linked arms with Amy as they
left in search of her luggage. "Actually it's a guest house.
I know the people, and they're delighted to rent the
place to you for a few months. They're a little tired of
having guests, anyway."

"That sounds terrific, Rhonda." Amy tried to pump
some enthusiasm into her voice.

"Did you get your car to the docks okay?"

"Yes, but I'll have to rent something until it arrives."

"Nonsense. I'll pick you up on my way in every day.
And if you have to take clients out, you can use my car
until yours gets here."

"Rhonda, I don't know how to thank you for all this."

Rhonda glanced at her. "You sound totally wiped
out, Amy."

Amy smiled wanly. "Long trip."

"In more ways than one, I bet." Rhonda patted her
arm. "Don't worry. You made the right decision."

"I certainly hope so."

"Life will look sweeter after a good night's sleep. I've
stocked the place with a few groceries, and you don't
have to come into the office until day after tomorrow."

"You're a peach, Rhonda."

"No, I'm a shrewd businesswoman. If you have the
potential I believe you do, my efforts to set you up here
will put money in both of our pockets."

"When do my real estate classes start?"

"Day after tomorrow."

"I see. I'd better take advantage of my one day off
tomorrow, right?"

"That's right," Rhonda said. "It may be your last for some time to come. That's the only way to make it in this business."

"That's okay with me. I want to work hard." *That way I'll have less time to think about Jack*, Amy concluded silently.

"Good. Then we'll get along fine," Rhonda said.

And they did. Rhonda was a hard taskmaster, but Amy found real estate fascinating and didn't mind working late hours and studying far into the night.

Her tiny guest house was on the edge of a cliff overlooking the sea, but Amy didn't have much time to enjoy the view. That suited her perfectly, because idle moments fostered thoughts of Jack. His wish that she remember their last night together in detail had come true, and if he'd wanted her to ache for him, he'd gotten that wish, too. Work was all that helped her ease the pain, and she threw herself into her new field with a vengeance.

She set a pattern of telephoning her parents once a week and following that with a call to Brad. Amy's mother always sounded as if she were balancing on the brink of disaster, but when Amy checked with Brad he continually assured her that their parents were doing fine. Amy decided the truth was somewhere in between, and she was anxious to end the separation so she could stop worrying about her mother and father's welfare.

The first hurdle was passing her licensing exam. Amy crammed facts and figures into her head and paced the floor each night, quizzing herself. She'd always hated taking tests, and this one created more pressure than any she'd ever encountered. Instead of a grade in a course at school, the results of the exam would affect how soon she could truly begin her new career. And to make matters worse, Rhonda expected her to pass the first time through.

She faced the test with sweaty palms and an aching head. The questions seemed too difficult, the time period too short, and Amy left the examining room with the conviction that she'd failed.

When Rhonda received the results, she and Amy were the only ones in the office. Rhonda walked up quietly to Amy's desk and sat down in one of the chairs reserved for clients.

Amy looked into the cool gray of her eyes and grimaced. "Flunked, didn't I?"

"Of course you didn't flunk. Your score was excellent, as I knew it would be."

"I passed? All right!" Amy punched the air with her fist and laughed. "And they said it couldn't be done."

"Oh? Who said that?"

Amy shrugged. "A few people. I wasn't exactly an A student in high school."

"That doesn't mean anything. You probably weren't motivated in high school."

"Not like this, I wasn't. Now if we could only get some nibbles on my property, I'd be on my way."

"You will. Have patience. And now, in the meantime, you can sell other people's property. Congratulations." Rhonda smiled warmly. "And welcome to this crazy business."

"Thanks. You've made everything possible. Thank goodness I at least have my car now."

"You'll be needing it for squiring all those hot prospects around. Listen, I think this calls for a celebration. When Bob and Carter come back, we'll see if they can make it for dinner tonight with their wives. My treat."

"I'd love that, Rhonda. But we can go Dutch."

"Nonsense. I write such things off my income tax, you know."

"All right." Amy laughed. "Once again, you make everything sound like a good business decision."

The evening was filled with boisterous fun, and Amy was surprised when she glanced at her watch to discover it was ten-thirty. "I'd better go home, Rhonda. Tomorrow's a work day."

Rhonda looked at her watch. "You're right. We'd all better leave. Amy, I just remembered that you might have wanted to call your family. Now it's too late."

"Yeah. Twelve-thirty is sort of late, I guess."

"I'm sorry, Amy."

"Don't worry about it. I can call them tomorrow night, Rhonda. I wouldn't have missed this party for anything."

As she drove home, Amy thought about tomorrow's phone call to her mother and father. But there was someone else she wanted to share the news with, someone who truly understood what she was going through.

Amy imagined Jack as he would be right now, sprawled in the bed where they'd made love the last night she was in Bellingham. Thinking of him lying there alone among the crumpled sheets brought a jolt of pain and longing.

Amy began to shake as the uncontrollable urge to hear Jack's voice overcame her. She didn't care what time it was in Bellingham. She hadn't contacted him since she'd left, but now, for the sake of her sanity, she had to make this call.

12

ONCE INSIDE the privacy of her little guest house, Amy tossed her new briefcase, a gift from Rhonda, on the kitchen table. Then she walked slowly into the small living room and stared at the telephone squatting on a low table beside the couch. She'd never considered calling Jack until tonight. She'd never had anything to say.

But passing her exam was the first tangible proof that she could make this crazy plan work. Ironically, every success she scored took her further away from Jack, and yet he was the one she longed to tell.

Maybe she hadn't completely given up the thought that if she proved herself, and her parents moved to Hawaii, Jack might reconsider his decision to live in Honolulu. He'd said that he didn't relish sacrificing his career for something that might not work out for her, but what if she pulled it off, became a successful agent?

Amy sank to the couch and pulled the telephone over into her lap. Thoughtfully she ran one finger along the top of the black phone's receiver. The glossy line through the dust testified to how little time she'd spent keeping house. But her single-mindedness had paid off. She'd passed the test.

She picked up the receiver and replaced it in the cradle. It was one o'clock in the morning in Bellingham. Common sense dictated that she wait until morning, but Amy didn't want to do that. She knew Jack had a phone in the bedroom. She wanted to talk to him while he was still slightly groggy from sleep, still stretched out in the bed she could picture so completely.

Was he wearing anything at all? Amy didn't really know what his sleeping habits were when he was alone. And she had no doubt that he was alone. She believed in his love, believed that he was waiting, as she was, to see how everything turned out. He hadn't given up, either.

She picked up the receiver again and began to punch in the numbers. But her hands were shaking and she hung up, sure she'd hit the wrong button by mistake. Now was not the time to reach a wrong number.

Amy took a deep breath and forced herself to dial slowly and carefully. The clicks of the various connections seemed to go on interminably before she finally heard a ring.

Amy cleared the lump from her throat as the phone rang again. And again. He had to be there. He just had to.

On the fourth ring he picked it up and mumbled a sleepy greeting.

"Jack, it's me, Amy."

"Amy?"

"Yes." She savored the sound of her name spoken in his rich voice, even if it was still husky with sleep.

"Are you all right? Amy, it's . . . it's one o'clock in the morning here. You're not in trouble, are you?"

"No, Jack. I just . . . just needed to hear your voice, and I called. I know what time it is there, but you see, I—"

"I know." His tone had become soft and intimate. "You wanted to talk to me while I was still in bed."

"Well . . ."

"I like that, Amy." His voice caressed her across the vast expanse of ocean. "I was dreaming about you."

"You'd say that even if you weren't."

"True. But I really was. It was an old dream, the one where you and I are in the grass hut, and we—"

"I remember." Amy's body grew taut with the familiar emotions he generated in her.

"I hope so. Mm, I wish you were right here in this bed with me. I can imagine several things we might do together."

Amy squirmed against the couch. "I—I think we'd better talk about something else."

"You're the one who called and woke me up."

"I know. Maybe that was a mistake."

"No, not a mistake. Your instincts are right on target. If I can't hold you in this bed, I might as well talk to you from it. Miss me?"

"Like you wouldn't believe."

"You didn't say goodbye."

"That's because I couldn't, Jack. Slipping away quietly was better for both of us."

"Better for you, maybe. I was a basket case when I woke up and found you gone. I wanted to kiss you once more, maybe even make love to you again before—"

"Jack, stop."

"Okay."

"How's the reading center coming along?"

"Terrific. A month ago we raised the last few thousand we needed, and I'm working with a contractor on the plans now."

"That's wonderful, Jack. How are Beeper and Steve?"

"Good. Steve wanted to write to you, but I told him I don't have your address. Which I don't, you know."

"I know. Have . . . have Steve ask my mom for it."

"How about Jack? Should he ask your mother, too?"

She winced at the sarcasm in his voice. "I didn't think I could handle polite little letters back and forth."

"Who said my letters would be polite?"

"You know what I mean, Jack. I don't want to be your pen pal."

"Then give me your phone number, Amy."

"No."

"That's not fair. You've got mine."

"Should I hang up?"

"No." He was quiet for a moment. "So how're things going over there?"

"That's really why I called. I passed my licensing exam. I'm a bona fide real estate lady now."

His response was a little slow in coming. "That's great news."

"You don't really want me to fail at this, do you?"

He sighed. "No, but if you succeed, you won't be coming home to stay, and I want that, too."

"Jack, this idea of mine isn't a flash in the pan. Now that I have my license, the only thing left is selling the land and buying something better for my parents. Rhonda thinks I'll do that, maybe in the next two or three months."

"Maybe you will."

"If that happens, I wondered if you'd reconsider. About moving here, I mean. I know you want to launch the reading center, but after that . . ."

"Moving to Hawaii doesn't make much sense for me, Amy. After you left and I was going a little crazy, I checked into jobs on Oahu, and the pay's not very good."

"Why not?"

"The station managers figure the scenery is part of the paycheck. That's fine if living there is what someone wants, but I'm not very excited about the idea. Besides that, a Seattle station is making noises as if they'd like to hire me. That would be my best career move, Amy, not tripping off to Hawaii and a pay cut."

And me, Amy thought, but she said nothing. If Jack didn't consider her presence worth more than money and a more prestigious job, then so be it.

"Amy, that didn't come out quite right."

"Sounded logical to me, Jack."

"Yes, and damned monetary, too. That's not all there is to this. I'm looking at all the factors. The idea of being tied to a place that isn't my first choice, because you can't leave your parents, seems a little out of whack, too. It's wonderful if they want to retire in Hawaii and can handle it on their own. But because they're dependent on you, that means you have to live there, and if I want to be near you, I have to live there."

"That about sums it up."

"Amy, your parents are controlling your life, and consequently mine."

"They're controlling mine by my own choice, and whether or not they affect yours is up to you."

"The hell it is! I'm in love with you. They've already affected my life, and I don't like it."

"Too bad, Jack. I didn't ask you to fall in love with me. If this is so inconvenient for you, why don't you just unfall yourself?"

"Sometimes I wish I could."

"Then do it."

"I can't, Amy. Dreaming of you tonight wasn't by chance. I dream of you every night. You've wormed your way inside me."

"But you won't come to Hawaii."

"I don't think it's a good idea."

"Then I guess this conversation is over. Have a nice day, Jack." She hung up before he could reply and put the telephone on the table with a clang. Then she covered her face with her hands and began to sob.

NO MORE PHONE CALLS to Jack, Amy decided the next day. Her system balked at functioning after a sleepless night, and she had to do well on the job, considering that was all she had right now. That and her obligation to get her parents to Hawaii.

Two months dragged by, and only a few people showed interest in the property on Maui. One man went so far as to fly over with her, but the long drive to Hana convinced him not to buy the lot.

Then one day while Amy was talking to a client on the phone, Rhonda put a listing on her desk for a condo in Honolulu. After she hung up, Amy read the note attached, recommending it as a spot for her parents.

She scanned the listing as she walked back to Rhonda's desk. "This sounds perfect—ocean view, three blocks from the beach, remodeled kitchen. But the price is over my head, Rhonda, even if I'd sold the Maui land, which I haven't."

Rhonda put down her pen. "There's more to the story. I took that listing personally, and the price is something the wife insisted on. I happen to know the husband wants to sell for less."

"How much less?"

"A third."

Amy whistled. "That would make it very attractive. Still steep, but I could manage."

"I was hoping you'd say that. Let's make them an offer."

"How? I don't have the money, and the wife will turn it down, won't she? You have to get both of them to agree if they both own the place."

"They'll agree. After I left them yesterday, the husband called me and explained that his wife always sets an unrealistically high price on everything, but when someone offers her less, she takes it. He really wants to sell. They both do."

"Why?"

"Island fever. They've been here five years."

"Oh." Amy looked at the paper in her hand. "Then this will probably be gone by the time I've sold my lot on Maui."

"Undoubtedly. Amy, let me put the money up. You'll sell that lot, and you can pay me back."

"I couldn't let you do that, Rhonda."

"Of course you could! You can't afford not to. This sort of deal won't come along again soon. Be aggressive, Amy. Learn to wheel and deal a little. Accept my offer in the spirit of a business venture, not a personal favor. If the worst happens and you never pay me for the condo, I'll turn around and sell it at a profit, so don't worry about me."

Amy grinned. "I would never worry about you, Rhonda. You're the most self-sufficient woman I know. And you manage to make every nice thing you do sound like a hardheaded business decision. But I still think your motivation is to help people, no matter what you say."

"I've found that helping people is often the best business decision anyone can make." Rhonda shrugged. "So who knows if I'm selfish or a saint? I'll leave that for you to decide, my young philosopher. Shall we make an offer on that condo?"

"Yes, right after I look at it."

Rhonda's gray eyes twinkled. "Good for you. And you should look at it. But I know you'll love the place."

"So do I, but my boss has taught me to form my own opinions about a situation."

"Wise lady."

"Yep."

Events moved quickly after that. The condo owners accepted the lower offer and the necessary paperwork was begun. The excitement of owning the condo fueled Amy's efforts to sell her Maui lot, and within two weeks she'd found a qualified buyer. The sale of her lot took place only days after the closing on the condo.

"I've done it!" Amy whirled jubilantly around in her desk chair after learning that the check for the lot had cleared the bank.

No one in the office had to ask what she'd done. Bob and Carter shouted their congratulations across the room, and each one stopped by her desk sometime during the day to tell her personally how happy they were for her. Amy basked in her success all day. By five o'clock, as was often the case, she and Rhonda were the only ones left in the office.

"So now what?" Rhonda asked, strolling to the front of the room. "Will you call your parents?"

"I've been thinking about how to handle this. There didn't seem much point in worrying about it until it happened, but now I need to decide." Amy leaned her chin on her hand. "This sort of thing should be done in person. They'll have to sell their house, for one thing, so they'll have that money to live on over here."

"How soon do you want to go?"

"As soon as I save the money for a round-trip ticket. That is, if you'll give me a week or so off to go back."

"You know I will, Amy. But with your tight budget, how will you save enough for the ticket?"

"Sell more real estate, I guess." Amy smiled. "Or go back to entering contests. I saw one the other day for a trip to Disneyland. That's sort of close."

"Not close enough." Rhonda sat on the edge of Amy's desk and thought for a minute. "I've got a better contest in mind."

"Oh? I didn't think you were into such things."

"Not contests based on luck. But sales contests are something else again. I've just decided to sponsor one in the office. The sales rep to bring in the most business by a week from tomorrow will win a trip to the city of his or her choice."

"Rhonda, you don't have to—"

Her boss held up one hand. "Save the protests. You may not win. You don't have the leads and contacts that Bob and Carter have. You'll have to work your little fanny off. But if you do it, you'll have commissions that should exceed the base salary I've started you on, and a free trip to boot."

"I'm going to win, Rhonda."

"You just might. You have two advantages. You're highly motivated, and you have one evening's head start. I won't announce the contest until tomorrow morning." She pushed away from the desk. "If I were you, I'd get out my phone book and start soliciting business."

"I will. You're terrific, Rhonda."

"I'm a businesswoman. Can you imagine how many sales we'll have in the next seven days while those two guys struggle to keep up with you?"

Amy pulled her telephone book from a drawer and plopped it on the desk. "They don't stand a chance."

"Oh, yes they do. They're both go-getters."

"And then there's me." Amy flipped open the book, cradled the receiver against her shoulder and started to dial. As she glanced up, she barely caught Rhonda's satisfied smile as her boss walked back to her desk.

13

DESPITE A WEEK of very little sleep, Amy faced the morning after the sales contest deadline with an exhilaration that she'd never experienced before. Even if she didn't win, she'd learned something priceless in the past few days that made the contest almost unimportant. She'd found out what Amy Hobson was supposed to do with her life.

No doubts lingered about her career choice. She belonged in sales, as Rhonda had predicted. Amy knew after the excitement of the week, the thrill of competing in the business world, that the future would bring enough financial success to do whatever she wanted, including settle her parents in Hawaii. If she didn't win the trip, she'd simply go out and earn enough to pay her own way.

Her confidence level was so high that when Rhonda announced her name as the top sales rep for the contest, she wasn't particularly surprised. She accepted the certificate amid enthusiastic applause from Rhonda, Carter and Bob.

As she looked around at the smiling faces, she realized that the other two agents in the office felt the same self-confidence she'd gained during the week of intense selling. They didn't begrudge her the victory, because they were already winners in their own right.

Later that day, Rhonda found a private moment to congratulate her.

"The funny thing is," Amy said, "that at the beginning of the contest I thought that I had to win. This morning I decided that it didn't matter."

Rhonda smiled knowingly. "I could tell. I'd hoped that's what would happen if you really poured on the steam. Success begets success, Amy. You won't need any special concessions from here on out. So when do you want to leave?"

"Next Saturday, if that's no problem for you. And I'll be back in two weeks, unless I can get my folks to wrap everything up sooner."

"You'll probably need two weeks. No problem. And let me know which flight you'll bring them in on. I'd like to meet you and give them a nice welcome. If the timing's right, we could arrange dinner."

"That sounds like a great idea." Amy hugged her impulsively. "I have so much to thank you for."

"But you've accomplished the hard part, Amy. You've done a lot of growing in the last few months. I'm very proud of you."

"I'm proud of myself, as a matter of fact."

"You should be. By the way, you never talk about that young man who came to Hawaii with you the first time. Are you still in touch with him?"

Amy shook her head. "Not really."

"I got the impression you liked him a lot."

"I still do, but there are . . . several problems."

"Would your recent successes help those problems or make them worse?"

Amy shuffled some papers on her desk. "I honestly don't know." She looked into Rhonda's gray eyes. "But maybe I should find out."

"Maybe you should."

Later that evening, when Amy thought Jack would be home from the station, she called his apartment. Instead of him, she reached a recording that said the number had been disconnected.

Disconnected? She sat for a moment in shock and outrage, until she remembered that she'd never given him any way to reach her. It was her own fault if now she didn't even know where to find him.

Or did she? He'd mentioned the possibility of a job in Seattle when she'd called him almost two months earlier. A call to directory assistance in Seattle confirmed her suspicion that he'd taken the job and moved to the large city.

Amy paced the floor and tried to decide whether or not to call him in Seattle. She looked again at the scribbled number. He'd begun a new life in a new city. Amy wondered if that meant that he had given up on them, after all.

Well, if he had, she wanted to hear him say so, to speak the words pronouncing the death of their relationship. Without that, she'd never quite believe that what they had shared was completely over. She picked up the receiver and dialed the Seattle number.

Jack answered on the second ring, and he sounded bright and alert. The big-city life must have been agreeing with him.

Amy took a deep breath. "Hi, Jack! How's your new job?"

"Amy? I'm so surprised to hear from you. I was expecting another . . . that is, someone else was supposed to . . ."

"A woman?" Amy pressed her lips together and swore at herself. "Forget I said that."

"Yes, a woman. She wanted to discuss some ideas for a teen literacy program here in Seattle. The station likes what I did in Bellingham and wants me to try the same thing here, only on a bigger scale."

"That's great, Jack." Amy's heart was doing tricky things inside her chest. This woman could be a business contact or his latest love interest, or both. And Amy had no right to ask anything more about her.

"So what are you up to, Amy?"

"I'm, uh, flying in on Saturday and going up to see the folks. You'll be on the way, so I wondered if you'd like to have a cup of coffee, talk over old times." She prayed that she sounded more casual than she felt.

"Flying in? How long will you be here?"

Amy wondered if her presence would louse up something he had going with the literacy lady. "About two weeks. Then the folks and I will all be coming back here."

"You found them something?"

"Yes."

"And sold the Maui lot?"

"Yes, I did."

"Fantastic. You must be turning into a super sales-lady to accomplish that little number. How did you manage to pull off what every real estate agent in Honolulu said couldn't be done?"

Amy drank in the pride she heard in his voice. "Well, I tried to make every aspect an advantage instead of a

disadvantage. I played up the idea of living where celebrities chose to live, away from the hubbub. Eventually I found a reclusive couple who loved testing their
four-by-four on the winding road and thought the black
sand was exotic."

"Good for you, Amy. What do your folks think of all
this?"

"I haven't told them. I'm planning it as a surprise and
hoping they'll be ecstatic once they get over the shock
of what I propose to them."

"I'm sure they will, Amy."

"Do you have time to see me for a little while? I'll be
renting a car, so I could meet you anywhere, near your
station or whatever."

"That's silly. I'll pick you up at the airport and drive
you to Bellingham. I've been meaning to go up and
check on the reading center progress, anyway."

"Jack, I'm sure you don't have time to—"

"Let me be the judge of that. In this job I happen to
have Saturday and Sunday off, and I'd be glad to take
you up there."

"O-Okay." Amy wondered what happened to all her
newfound confidence when it came to Jack. With clients
she was firm and decisive. With Jack she sounded like
a tentative kid again. "I mean, that's fine, Jack. Let me
give you my flight number and arrival time."

"You do that."

Amy reached in her briefcase for the tickets she'd
picked up from the travel agency after work. In a businesslike manner, she read off the information printed
on the ticket. "So I'll see you then," she said briskly.

"Amy?"

"What?"

"You're a pip, you know that?"

"I can't imagine what you mean."

"I think you can. Goodbye, Amy."

FIVE MONTHS, Amy thought as she walked through the narrow throat of the connecting ramp between the plane and the waiting room. She knew how she had changed, but she didn't know much of anything about what had happened to Jack in that time. Her short conversation with her parents, in which she'd told them Jack would be bringing her up to Bellingham, hadn't produced much news.

Her mother had insisted Jack stay with them the one night he'd be in Bellingham. She mentioned how considerate Jack had been while Amy had been gone, how he'd come to say goodbye before he left for Seattle and had given her his new address and telephone number in case they had needed him for anything. Amy wondered if Jack had intended that the information be passed on to Hawaii. If so, her mother hadn't said anything about Jack's leaving or his new job, and Amy wasn't sure why.

Maybe her mother thought that without Jack, Bellingham wouldn't hold any appeal for Amy whatsoever and she'd never come home. The thought of Bellingham without Jack in it was rather dismal, but considering the changes Amy was about to make, who lived in the town and who didn't no longer mattered.

For this first meeting with Jack after so many months apart, Amy had deliberately chosen her new pink suit. The outfit presented her exactly as she wanted Jack to see her—still feminine but with a new sense of purpose and direction. She'd left her hair loose around her shoulders because Jack had a weakness for her unfettered hair, even though a more controlled style might have fitted the image better. Amy didn't mind playing on any weaknesses she could find.

She stepped out of the passageway and into the waiting room. She faltered in her stride as she searched the group of people for Jack. Then she saw him, back a little from the others, dressed in a sport jacket and a loosened tie, his hands in the pockets of his slacks. The impression he made was the exact counterpart to hers—businesslike yet masculine.

He had seen her, too. She could tell from the widening of his eyes, the slight movement in her direction before he seemed to remember that he wanted to appear casual. Amy didn't care how he wanted to appear. She couldn't get to him fast enough.

"Jack, it's so good to see you." She was smiling like an idiot as she stood before him, but she couldn't help it.

He rocked back on his heels and assessed her carefully. "You look wonderful, Amy."

"Mom wants you to stay with us tonight. She said you could have Brad's old room."

His blue eyes searched her face. "All right."

Amy stood there uncertainly. "Have you...got a hug for an old friend?"

"Sure." His arms came around her in a brotherly fashion.

Something in Amy rebelled at his impersonal touch, and without considering the consequences, she wound her arms around his neck and kissed him full on the lips. She felt his jolt of reaction and the tightening of his grip.

She grew dizzy with excitement as he answered her kiss with unexpected force. He still loved her!

When they drew apart, they were both flushed and unsteady. They stood for a minute staring at each other in silence.

"So," Jack said softly, "that's how it is."

"Afraid so, Jack. Who's the lady you were expecting that call from?"

"Nobody. I've tried to be interested in other women. It's a waste of time. I've got this thing for some wahine living in Hawaii. How about you?"

"I don't even date. I can't imagine holding someone else's hand, or kissing—"

He gripped her arms. "I sure hope not. When I think of you with another guy, I become slightly murderous."

"Don't worry." She smiled up at him. "It won't happen."

He shook his head. "This is the damnedest situation, Amy. Here I've got this new job in Seattle, and you're selling real estate like hotcakes in Honolulu. Where's the answer?"

"I don't know."

He looped an arm around her shoulder and led her toward the baggage area. "Will I be able to see you at all while you're over here? I mean alone?"

"You mean 'alone' alone?"

"You know good and well what I mean. And you're responsible, strutting around in that sexy little pink suit. Do we have to drive up to Bellingham today?"

"I'm afraid so."

"You're no fun, Amy. My new apartment has a beautiful view of Puget Sound," he coaxed.

Amy laughed. "Must be the Soundview Apartments."

"Smart aleck. Come on, let's call your folks and tell them we'll arrive tomorrow. Stay with me tonight."

She sighed and nestled against him as they walked. "I can't, Jack. I have to get up there right away. Moving them out of Bellingham in two weeks will be difficult enough without losing a day in the beginning."

"You're going to be a busy lady, then." He sounded hurt.

"Maybe not quite that busy," she said soothingly. "But if I can manage a free day, I'll have to drive down to Seattle to see you. I'd feel strange if we were to do anything . . . like that in my folks' house."

"I understand. So would I. What if I stay in a motel tonight and—"

"No. They'd be crushed. Mom seemed really excited about having you as a guest."

"Okay. But dammit, you look luscious."

"You're not so bad yourself. Is the sport coat and tie the new image for the big Seattle deejay?"

Jack grinned. "Yeah, I guess. I don't do as much of the sweatshirt-and-suspender routine these days. Besides, I'm getting a little old for that."

"My goodness, Jack. Are we growing up?"

"Looks that way."

"Before you know it, we'll be having garage sales and attending P.T.A. meetings."

"Correct me if I'm wrong, Amy, but don't you have to have kids to belong to the P.T.A.?"

"Well, sure. I just meant—"

"What did you mean?"

She looked into his eyes, so full of longing. "Nothing, Jack. Nothing, really."

"Dammit," he said softly, and looked away.

They spent the ride to Bellingham reviewing what had happened to each of them in the five months they'd been apart. Amy learned that Beeper had graduated and been given Jack's old job at KPLY. Steve, soon to be a senior, had taken over the schoolwork syndicate and was considering a career in the stock market. Both were reading above a sixth-grade level.

After they arrived at the Hobson house, Amy's father dragged Jack off to watch television, and Amy's mother related guilt-inducing tales of how many problems they'd had because she hadn't been in town to help in little ways.

"But Brad kept telling me how great everything was going," Amy protested.

"I wouldn't tell Brad my problems," Amy's mother replied. "He has enough to worry about with his own family."

Something clicked in Amy's head. Brad was allowed off the hook because he had a family. What if Amy suddenly announced she and Jack were getting married, that they intended to start a family? Would Amy's mother be forced to deal with her own problems on a permanent basis?

But Amy couldn't make that announcement. No matter how much he still cared for her, Jack hadn't offered to move to Hawaii to be with her. He resented the entanglement her parents represented, and Amy, out of the situation for five months, was beginning to see his point.

Her irritation didn't last, however, when she pictured the joy on her parents' faces when she told them about the condo on Oahu that was to be theirs. She couldn't give them a better gift in the world, and they deserved it. They would have provided it for themselves if Philip hadn't wiped out their savings.

She saved her announcement for the dinner table, between the main course and dessert. When her mother stood up to clear away the plates, Amy put a hand on her arm. "Just a minute, Mom. I have a surprise for you and Dad. I'd like to tell you about it now."

"A surprise?" Amy's mother sat down slowly and sent a knowing glance toward her husband. "This has something to do with Jack, doesn't it?"

"No, as a matter of fact. This has to do with you and Dad, and your dream of retiring in Hawaii."

Her father snorted. "That's a dream, all right. After Philip's little trick."

"Virgil, now we're not going to—"

"It's okay, Mom. Dad's right. Philip ruined your chances of retiring in Hawaii, and I feel responsible for bringing him into the picture."

Her father fidgeted with his spoon. "So what's this surprise?"

Amy paused and smiled. "You will be able to retire in Hawaii, after all. I've bought you a condo in Honolulu."

Her father's spoon clattered to his plate. "You did what?"

"I've been saving for some time, Dad. That's why I took the real estate job in Hawaii, to find something for both of you. It's not quite paid for, but with the way my commissions are mounting up, that shouldn't be a problem for much longer."

Her mother opened her mouth twice before she managed a whispered comment. "A condo in Hawaii?"

"It's beautiful, Mom. I've got pictures in my room. I'll be right back." She dashed from the table and ran up the stairs to find the snapshots she'd tucked away in her suitcase.

After she was gone, Virgil Hobson looked at Jack. "Did you know about this?"

"She told me a few months ago. Everything she's done—winning the trip last February, taking this job— all of it's been to try and get you two over there and make up for what happened with your savings."

Her mother shook her head. "And I thought she wanted to get away from us."

"Exactly the opposite," Jack said. "She plans to live in Honolulu with you. She's got it all figured out."

Virgil cleared his throat. "I don't know what to say. She's surprised me, all right. I never thought that Amy—"

"She's grown up, Mr. Hobson. She's not the scatterbrained kid she used to be."

"Did she tell Brad?"

"No." Jack smiled wryly. "She was afraid Brad would make fun of her for trying. She wanted to prove to him, and to you, that she could do this."

Her mother massaged her forehead. "I still can't believe it."

Amy hurried into the dining room with several snapshots in her hand. She gave them to her mother first. "That's your view from the lanai. And the next picture shows the front of the place. Look at all those flowers, Mom! And here's the kitchen. See how new it looks? The owners just remodeled last year."

Amy stood by anxiously while her mother sorted through the photographs and handed them to her father. "The whole place was just painted, Dad. And because it's a condo, the maintenance is minimal. How would you like to give up mowing lawns forever?"

"Oh, the lawn isn't so much trouble." Her father gazed at the last picture before putting the whole stack beside his plate. "Very nice place, Amy."

"I know you'll both love it. I managed to get two weeks off from work, which should be enough time to put this house on the market and get you all packed. I'd advise selling most of the furniture and buying some new things over there. The square footage is much less, for one thing, and—"

"Two weeks?" Amy's father stared at her. "You expect us to be packed and on a plane in two weeks?"

"Why not? That's enough time to give notice at work, and we can have a big garage sale next weekend. The house won't sell by then, of course, but we can finalize that through the mail. My being in real estate should simplify everything."

Amy's mother stood up. "Virgil, could I talk with you a minute? Alone?"

"Okay." Her father shoved back his chair and walked into the living room with his wife trailing behind.

Amy sank to her chair and looked across the table at Jack. "They're a little stunned, but they'll be okay."

"Sure they will." Jack reached across the white tablecloth and took her hand. "They need some time, that's all. You've done a wonderful thing for them, Amy."

"Do you think they liked the condo?"

"I think they're overwhelmed, and they haven't really absorbed the idea of living there, but they'll like it. From everything you've said, the place is perfect for someone who's always dreamed of living in Hawaii."

"It really is, Jack. Rhonda gets credit for discovering the property, though."

"Don't give away too much credit. You've done one hell of a job."

"Thanks, Jack." Amy squeezed his hand. Until her parents had recovered enough to show their gratitude, Jack's praise kept her spirits up.

Amy's parents returned from the living room and sat down at the table. Both of them appeared upset.

"Well," Amy said with a little laugh, "have you figured out what to keep and what to get rid of around here?"

"Nope." Her father wadded up his napkin and smoothed it out on his lap again. Then he took a drink of cold coffee and cleared his throat. He didn't look at her. "The fact is," he said, glancing furtively at his wife, "we don't want to go."

14

AMY REELED. "Wait a minute, Dad. You always said—"

"I know what I've said, Amy. And I always thought retiring in Hawaii was what I wanted. Until now, that is, when you announced that we'd have to leave in two weeks."

"If that's the problem, don't worry about the two weeks," Amy said quickly. "I can go back to Honolulu and you can follow me later. I thought it would be fun to go together, but two weeks is rushing you. I can see that now."

Amy's mother put a hand on her arm. "It's not just the two weeks, Amy. We don't want to leave Bellingham. We like this house. We're used to living here. Your father has a job he likes, and he might not find something in Hawaii."

"He's not supposed to find something. He's supposed to retire." Amy began to panic. All her plans, and now her parents didn't want to move? Making their dream come true was turning into a nightmare.

"Retire and do what, Amy?" Her father shrugged. "Sit on the lanai and enjoy the view all day? Watch television? You said the condo wouldn't require much maintenance. I'd go crazy with nothing to do."

"Then we'll find you a job. I'll take care of that. Dad, the weather is beautiful. No more cold, gray skies. Even the rain is warm, and you'll never see snow. And Mom, no more heating bills, no more winter coats. Wouldn't you love to get rid of all your heavy things?"

Her mother gave Amy a sad look. "I'm used to Bellingham now. I know the neighbors, and where the stores are. I'd have to make all new friends and learn about a whole new city. I'm comfortable here, Amy."

"I can't believe this." Amy threw her napkin on the table. "What am I supposed to do now?"

"Sell the condo," her mother said, "and come back home. We need you here, Amy. You know what a struggle I've had without you."

Amy glanced at Jack, but his expression told her nothing. He wouldn't try to influence her one way or the other, but he had to be wishing the same thing her mother was. "I can sell the condo," Amy said in a monotone, "but I can't come home. Not for another eighteen months, anyway. I signed a contract with Rhonda, my boss, agreeing to stay for a minimum of two years."

Her mother put a hand over her heart. "Two years! You didn't tell us that before."

"That's because I planned to bring you over long before then. In fact, I'm right on schedule. I hoped to have everything arranged in less than six months, and here I am. And all for nothing."

Jack spoke for the first time. "Not for nothing, Amy. You've got a career in real estate."

"Yeah, you're right." She laughed. "Funny, isn't it? My whole motivation was to help my parents, and now I'm the only one who benefits from all this. I can't win with you guys, can I?"

Her father's voice was gruff with emotion. "Of course you can. We appreciate everything you've done. Maybe you should have consulted with us first, but your heart was in the right place."

"Great." She slapped the table and stood up. "Little Amy's heart was in the right place. Well, if you'll excuse me, I have a call to make. Rhonda wanted me to let her know as soon as possible when you'd be arriving, so she could plan a big welcoming party. I might as well tell her to forget the plan and put the condo on the market."

Dangerously close to tears, Amy turned and bolted up the stairs to her room. She'd rather make this call from the privacy of her bedroom phone.

Knowing Rhonda probably was still at the office, Amy tried there first. Bob answered, and when he recognized Amy's voice, told her he'd get Rhonda right away. Amy sighed. They'd all been so supportive. How could she face them with the news that her parents had thrown this marvelous gift back in her face?

"How's my super saleslady?"

Amy's eyes filled with tears at Rhonda's cheerful greeting. "Not so great, Rhonda. My parents turned thumbs down on the condo."

"They don't like it? I was sure they would. Well, maybe we can sell that and find another—"

"No, I mean they don't want to move to Hawaii at all. They've decided Bellingham is where they want to retire."

"Oh, Amy." Rhonda's sympathy stretched across the distance between them. "You had such wonderful plans for all of you to be here together."

Amy tried to steady her voice. "So much for plans."

"Didn't you say that your father's disabled? I thought that was part of the reason you needed to live close to them."

"Well, yes, it was."

"And now they don't want to move."

"That's what they said."

"Do you think they'll change their minds, Amy?" Rhonda's tone was gentle.

"I don't know. But if I have to talk them into the idea, and then they don't like it once everything is settled, then—"

"I see your point. They've got to be wholeheartedly in favor of the move or you'll be blamed if anything goes wrong. I agree. Coaxing them to come over here would be a big mistake." Rhonda sighed. "What an unfortunate situation. How will they manage for the next eighteen months without you?"

"I'm not sure, but they'll have to figure something out, I guess."

Rhonda didn't reply right away. Finally she spoke with no trace of bitterness. "Consider your contract null and void, Amy. I can't hold you here under these circumstances. If your family needs you, then I'll release you from your obligation to me."

"I can't let you do that, Rhonda. Not after all the training and the consideration you've given me."

"Yes, you can. Situations change. Had you known your parents had no intention of retiring in Hawaii, you'd never have entered into an agreement with me in the first place, correct?"

"That's true, I suppose."

"Then I'd have to be a real shark to force you into staying in Honolulu."

"What happened to the hardheaded business-woman, Rhonda?"

"Oh, I'm not as mushy as you think. You wouldn't make a very good employee if you were worried about your parents every minute."

"But I managed and they managed for almost six months."

"Yes, but you called them every week, and you knew the time would be short. The truth is, I'd rather you didn't take off after eighteen months are up, either. I'd like to see you hang around long enough to build a real career for yourself. But under these circumstances, you won't be thinking that way."

"Probably not." For the first time Amy felt a twinge of resentment against her parents. What Rhonda was describing, a chance to build on her success in the atmosphere of support Rhonda provided, sounded like a fine opportunity. But her parents needed her to stay closer to home.

"Go on, Amy. Tell your folks you'll be coming home for good. Fly back here whenever you can, and I'll help you tie up the loose ends and get back on the plane to Washington. You can sell real estate there, too, you know. You've got enough talent to make it anywhere."

Amy took a deep breath. "Thanks for everything, Rhonda. As always, you've been there when I needed you. I'll let you know when I'm flying in."

"Fine. And don't worry. Things will work out. You'll see."

Amy descended the stairs with her thoughts in a jumble. Her mother and father would be delighted with the news, of course. And Jack. Wouldn't her release from her contract mean that she had a future with Jack? Apparently she could have it all—career, family approval and the man she loved—for the small price of cancelling Rhonda's contract. And Rhonda was willing to cancel it.

When she reentered the dining room, her mother had cleared away the main course and was bringing out slices of chocolate cake. Jack and her father were discussing the chances of the Seattle Seahawks making it to the Super Bowl. How could they act so normal, she wondered, when her entire world was in turmoil?

Jack looked up first and turned toward her. "Did you get Rhonda?"

"Yes. She said that under the circumstances she would release me from my two-year contract."

Both Amy's parents exclaimed about the wonderful news, but Amy watched Jack's eyes to gauge his reaction.

At first they lit with excitement, but then he seemed to make a conscious effort to control the expression on his face. "What are you going to do?" he asked calmly.

"Why, she's coming home, of course," her mother said with a delighted smile. "Amy, this must be fate. You had to go over there to discover what career was right for you, and now you can sell real estate in Bellingham." She glanced furtively at Jack. "Or Seattle, maybe. That's not very far away, really."

"No, not very far," Amy agreed, still looking at Jack.

His blue eyes remained unreadable. "Then you're canceling the contract?"

"I guess I am."

Slowly the muscles in his face relaxed, and he smiled at her. "Just wanted to be sure."

"Oh?" She raised an eyebrow. "Why?"

"We can discuss it later. In fact, I planned to drive down to the station and check on old Beeper tonight.

Want to come along? Steve said he'd be there, and he wanted me to bring you."

"That would be nice." Amy's heart pounded as she sat down in her chair and took a bite of cake that she couldn't taste. What would she and Jack discuss later? She could think of only one subject. The possibility of making a commitment to Jack, of planning a life together, made her dizzy with anticipation. She wanted him so much, and now he was within reach.

Half an hour later Jack tucked her in the car and drove toward the bay. Because of daylight saving time, the sun, orange as a melon ball, was just setting against the horizon.

"This isn't the way to the station," Amy commented.

"We have plenty of time to get there before ten. I thought you might like to watch the sunset from this side of the ocean for a change."

"Okay." She glanced at his profile, his dark hair ruffled by the breeze from the open car window. His blue shirt was open at the collar; his hands rested lightly on the steering wheel, but the intent set of his mouth belied his casual appearance.

Jack parked so they could look out over the water and watch the sun slowly dip into the sea. "You've got to admit this isn't such a bad place to live."

"I never said it was. Especially in the summer, when it's warmer and doesn't rain much. Maybe if I'd asked my folks to move in February I would have gotten a different reaction."

"I don't think so." He turned to look at her.

"Neither do I. They've changed their minds about Hawaii. Unfortunately, they didn't realize it until I gave them the chance to move there."

Jack took her left hand and began stroking her fingers. "You've been through the meat grinder on this. I know how much you wanted to make their dream real, and how hard you've worked, what you've sacrificed. . . ."

"We've both had to sacrifice, Jack."

"Yes, we have." He caressed her ring finger. "And the time has come to stop sacrificing, Amy." His blue eyes gazed steadily at her. "Marry me."

She began to tremble, even though she'd been expecting the question. She would remember this moment for the rest of her life, remember how the orange sun cast a warm glow over everything—the water, the boats at anchor, Jack's face, so full of love.

He touched her cheek. "You look a little dazed. Shall I repeat the question?"

Amy nodded. "I love hearing it," she whispered.

"That's nice to know." He smiled gently. "Please marry me, Amy Hobson. Share my life; share my bed, and together we'll prove that the beans-in-a-jar theory is a lot of nonsense." His voice became husky. "I love you so much."

"And I love you," Amy replied dreamily. "Of course I'll marry you."

His kiss was as warm as the setting sun. Amy moaned and locked her fingers at the nape of his neck to hold him close as she and Jack tasted the promised sweetness of commitment.

As the kiss became more passionate, Jack cupped her breast and tried unsuccessfully to maneuver around the console between them. At last he lifted his head and chuckled in frustration. "I love this car, but not for kissing you. Where can we go?"

"Nowhere, Jack." Amy smiled up at him. "We've got an appointment with Beeper and Steve, remember?"

"And then we have to go back to your house and sleep in separate bedrooms," Jack said with a grimace.

"Yes, but I have a plan. I'll go back with you tomorrow but I won't make a plane reservation until Monday. It won't be necessary to explain all that to my parents, and we can have one night alone before I fly back."

His blue gaze was fierce. "How soon can you come home for good?"

"With Rhonda's help, very soon."

"That's good. Now that you've said yes, I don't think I can wait very long before we make it official. God, I want you." He kissed her again, and when they parted both were breathing hard.

"I think we'd better go to the station," Amy said, pushing gently on his chest. "Beeper will be very disappointed if you don't show up. I'm sure he's proud of his new position."

"You're right. But I'd much rather find the nearest motel and take you to bed."

"The timing's wrong. Tomorrow will be here before you know it."

"I doubt that." Jack straightened his clothes and put the key into the ignition. "But I guess I shouldn't be greedy. Two hours ago I thought I might never make love to you again."

Amy squeezed his arm. "Life wouldn't be that cruel to us."

He smiled at her. "Apparently not. Let's go see how Beeper's manning that microphone."

A few minutes later Amy stood with Steve outside the control booth and watched Beeper and Jack do an impromptu comedy routine for the benefit of the KPLY listeners.

Beside Amy, Steve beamed with pride. "Beeper's great, isn't he?"

"Yes, he is, but you're pretty great yourself, Steve. How long ago did you change your image?"

"You like it? I don't look like a geek? Nobody at school recognizes me, hardly."

"I can see why."

"You didn't like the purple hair, did you?"

"It was ... distinctive, but I doubt you could have gotten away with purple hair in the financial world."

"Yeah, how about that? My grades are coming up, slow but sure, and with a little luck I can get into Western and take some business courses."

"That's terrific, Steve."

Steve ran a hand over his crew cut. "It all started one day when Beeper dragged me along when he had to take something to his parents' stockbroker. I was blown away by all that—the Dow Jones Average, stock market news flashing across their computer screens, calls from New York and junk like that.

"I told Beeper 'That's for me,' and he said 'Go for it, but first we've got to fix you up.' Then he took me for a haircut and bought me some clothes. He'd tried to do that before, but I'd never let him. This time I did, but I kept records. I'll pay him back someday. We drew up a contract, just like you had me sign last year."

Amy stared at him in amazement. She'd never heard Steve make such a long speech before. The change in him was phenomenal.

"Oh, and I've got a girlfriend," Steve added shyly.

Amy smiled. "Is she cute?"

"She's not just cute, she's hot, man. But I told her I had to get my career going before we talk about anything serious between us."

"That's very wise." Amy was so happy and proud that she wanted to hug him, but she doubted he'd appreciate the gesture.

"So what's happening with you in Hawaii? Jack told us the other day that you were just here for a visit."

"I was supposed to be, but now it looks like I may be moving back to Washington permanently."

"Hey, that's great, but how come? Jack said you'd be over there at least two years. At least I think that's what he said right after you left. Something about a lady training you to sell real estate if you'd stay for two years."

"Yes, well, that was the original agreement." Amy shifted her weight nervously. "But the woman's letting me out of it."

"Oh. You probably didn't sign anything, right? Otherwise she'd make you stay, I bet."

Amy looked away from the honesty in the young boy's eyes. "Actually, I did sign something, but the circumstances changed, and she offered to cancel the contract."

"You signed a contract?"

"Yes."

"But you have to live up to it, don't you?"

"Usually, yes. But this case is different."

Steve shook his head. "Boy, I thought signing a contract was real important. Putting your name on the line and everything."

Amy didn't reply as her words came back to haunt her. She had no answer for what Steve was saying, and his comments made her feel very uncomfortable. She gazed into the control booth where Jack and Beeper were laughing about some reaction from a listener who had phoned in. Jack glanced at Amy and caught her staring at him. He winked and blew her a kiss. She waved back and smiled brightly, but inside her uneasiness grew.

After she and Jack left the station he suggested a drive to some secluded spot so that they could be alone.

"I'd rather not, Jack. I'm really tired," Amy replied. "It's been a very long day."

"Yeah, you're right. But once we're inside the door of your folks' house, I won't even get to kiss you properly. Or should I say improperly. This is going to be one hell of a night, with you right down the hall."

"Parking somewhere for a few minutes won't help, Jack."

"I wish I had some sleeping pills," he grumbled, but he steered the car obediently in the direction of the Hobson house. As he helped Amy out of the car, Jack paused to look at the frayed basketball hoop hanging over the garage door. "The old hoop hasn't given up the ghost yet. Can you still make that hook shot I taught you?"

Amy chuckled. "I don't know."

"Hey, that's an idea. We could play a little b-ball and tire ourselves out."

"The neighbors might not appreciate that at this hour and we'd wake my folks."

Jack slid his arm around her waist and pulled her close. "I'd give a lot for a little one-on-one about now."

"So would I, but this isn't the time."

"I know, dammit."

They entered the darkened house quietly and tiptoed upstairs together. At the top of the landing Jack drew her toward him and covered her mouth in a silent, desperate kiss. Spreading his hands across her bottom, he urged her against his groin.

She resisted and drew her lips away from his. "Don't," she whispered.

"I'm going crazy, Amy," he murmured.

"I know. Me too. But we couldn't make love quietly after all this time, and you know it." She wiggled out of his arms. "Go to bed, Jack. I'll see you in the morning."

"Right. I'll be the one with eyes like a road map."

Amy laughed. "Me too. Good night. I love you."

"Prove it."

"Jack, that's the oldest line in the book. Besides, I already have proven it."

"I know, and that's what's driving me berserk. I remember how well you prove everything."

"Good night, Jack."

He sighed. "Good night, Amy."

For Amy, the night was a hundred years long. Sexual frustration was only part of her problem. The real issue that kept her tossing and turning was far more critical than one night of celibacy.

Steve's reaction to her canceled contract was to be expected, considering the emphasis she'd placed on the binding nature of contracts in general. The trouble was, she believed what she'd taught Steve. Rhonda deserved to have that agreement honored, and for Amy's own sense of worth, she needed to honor it, as well.

But what of her parents? Amy remembered Brad's favorable reports about how they were faring while she'd been gone. Amy herself had found no evidence of any hidden disasters in the few hours she'd been home. Could Brad have been right? Even before she'd left for Hawaii, he'd said that he didn't like the way their mother and father were tying Amy to them. But all along, she had allowed it to happen. Maybe she'd needed them to need her.

However, her success in Hawaii had changed that. Now her parents' dependency gave her a feeling of heaviness instead of satisfaction. Amy wanted to be free to pursue her own goals. The more she thought about it, the more Amy wondered if separating herself from her mother and father might be better for all of them.

That left Jack. She'd told him only hours before that she'd be his wife. And oh, how she wanted to be! The thought of waking up next to him every morning sent goose bumps prickling over her skin. She wanted to have children with him, to share everything from romantic dinners to broken plumbing. She loved him almost beyond reason. Almost.

But reason told her that she would always feel her happiness with Jack came at the price of her honor, that she'd taken the easy way, blaming it on her parents' decision not to move.

Amy propped her aching head on her fist and looked at the luminous dial of the clock radio beside the bed. Five o'clock in the morning. She threw back the rumpled covers and walked barefoot across the cold floorboards. Opening her door, she padded down the hall to Brad's old room.

She turned the knob and slipped inside without knocking. "Jack?"

His response came quickly, as if he'd only been dozing. "Amy. Come here, you. I didn't think you'd stay down there all night."

"No, Jack. That's not why I'm here. I'm going back to Hawaii."

"I know that, but only for a little while. It won't be much fun, but—"

"No, I mean I'm going back to honor the contract. I'm staying the full two years, Jack."

15

"WAIT A MINUTE." Jack snapped on the bedside light and rubbed his eyes. Then he blinked once and stared at her. "Repeat that, please."

Amy swallowed hard. He looked so damned sexy with the sheet draped across his hips and his chest bare and inviting. Was she out of her mind to make this decision? "Steve and I had a conversation while you were in the control booth with Beeper. We discussed contracts. Steve reminded me of something I already knew but had chosen to forget. I gave my word to Rhonda, and I intend to keep it."

"You gave your word to me, too," he said quietly. "You agreed to be my wife."

"That's true. And I want to marry you. But I didn't promise to stay in Washington."

His blue gaze became icy with anger. "That was understood. You knew that's why I made sure you would accept Rhonda's offer to let you out of the contract before I said anything."

Amy clenched her hands at her sides. "The fact remains that you didn't specify where we would live as part of your proposal. We can still be married. I'll stand by that decision. But I'll be in Hawaii for the next eighteen months, at least."

"At *least*?"

"If my career really takes off there, I may stay longer. The next eighteen months will satisfy my moral obligation to Rhonda, but I owe it to myself to find out how good I can be at this. I'll have built a reputation after two years, and I'd be a fool to quit and come running back, just because . . . just because . . ."

"Because you loved someone?" Jack finished bitterly. "Heaven forbid that you'd make a sacrifice for that reason."

"You're twisting this around to make it sound as if I don't really care about you, Jack, and that's not true. Please try to understand. You've always known what you wanted to do with your life, and you've made progress in your career. I'm in the process of discovering what I can do. I don't want to shortchange myself now."

"All right, forget about me. I thought you were convinced that your parents couldn't function for long without you. What's happened to that concern?"

"I've agonized over that situation, and when the answer came to me early this morning, I knew I had to go back to Hawaii."

"I don't get it."

"I've finally realized that I've encouraged them to be dependent on me because that was the only thing making me feel useful. Because I don't need their dependence anymore, I can see that they've managed just fine in the past six months. Brad kept telling me so, but I wouldn't believe it, didn't want to believe it, until recently."

Jack swung his feet over the edge of the bed and leaned his head in his hands. "That's something, anyway. I agree with you there." He looked up with a pleading expression. "But why go back to Hawaii, Amy? Rhonda's willing to let you go. Build your exciting career in Seattle, where we can be together. Don't shove this obstacle between us, just when we've found each other at last."

"Don't you see, Jack? Rhonda's willing to let me go because she thinks my parents require my care. Now that I know they don't, I'd be canceling the contract on a false premise. I can't do that."

"Can't or won't?"

"Won't."

"Amy, for God's sake!"

"Jack, if you were my friend, you would understand this."

"I'm not your friend, dammit! I'm the man who loves you so much I can't see straight!"

"I think you just said it all, Jack." She turned toward the door. "I'm going to get dressed, and then I'll go down and talk to Mom and Dad. Will you still drive me to the airport or should I rent a car?"

"I'll drive you. And I'd advise you to get a flight out today."

"I thought that's what you'd want."

"It is."

Amy opened the door and closed it carefully after her. Not until she was safely under the shower did she allow the sobs to come.

THE RIDE TO THE AIRPORT was the most difficult three hours Amy had spent in her life. She and Jack said goodbye without touching, and she practically ran down the corridor to the waiting plane. She drank cocktails all the way to Honolulu and splurged on a cab to take her home. Rhonda didn't know she was arriving, and that was fine with Amy. All she wanted was to be alone.

On the second day of her self-imposed exile she called Rhonda, explained that she was back and invited her boss to lunch. Over salads and wine Amy poured out the entire miserable story.

"So I'm here to finish out the contract, if you'll have me," Amy said, swallowing the last of her wine.

"Of course I'll have you, but shouldn't you go home to that man of yours? I can see how much you love him, Amy."

"Unfortunately. But if he couldn't understand the importance of my coming back here, we'd never make it, Rhonda. He has to respect my principles."

"Having principles can be very lonely, sweetheart."

"So I'm finding out." Amy lifted her chin. "But being with him, and having an uneasy feeling that I wasn't being true to myself, would have been worse. I may be lonely, but I feel good about my decision."

"Well, that's the bottom line, I guess." Rhonda smiled reassuringly. "You'll be okay, as long as you keep busy. I've had a couple of nibbles on your condo."

"Let's take it off the market."

"Why?"

"Because if I'm going to stay, I might as well buy as pay rent, wouldn't you say?"

"Really putting down roots, aren't you?"

"That's exactly what I'm doing, and I'm going to bloom and grow, Rhonda."

Rhonda squeezed her hand. "You're already doing that. Congratulations."

AMY FOUND that the condo suited her perfectly. She developed the habit of having her dinner on the lanai every evening she didn't have appointments. She'd watch the water and the lights, and the moon if it was shining. Once in a while a moonbow would appear, and she'd force herself to look at it with dry eyes.

When her finances improved, she splurged on some stereo equipment. One day in a record store she stumbled on her favorite Simon and Garfunkel album and bought it impulsively. She discovered that playing "Bridge Over Troubled Water" was like pressing on an aching tooth. Touching the soreness hurt, but leaving it alone hurt more.

She made friends with a neighbor, a widow who seemed to need occasional company as much as Amy. Sometimes Amy invited Edith over for an evening chat, and they'd sit on the lanai together and share bits from their past. Eventually Amy told her new friend about Jack. Edith was a good listener, and Amy discovered that talking about the man she loved, but couldn't have, was a kind of therapy.

As Amy's business increased, she spent more evenings with clients than at home and the lanai often stood empty. She was almost too busy to decorate her new home, but she managed to squeeze in time to shop for rattan furniture that complemented the tropical look that she'd grown to love. The couch and chairs were softened with plump cushions in a bold Hawaiian print and the tabletops were all made of sparkling glass.

One Saturday Amy bought as many green plants as she could stuff in her car and brought them home. But her life was too hectic to spend time caring for the plants, and they began to wilt. Finally, in desperation, she gave Edith a key and begged her to take on the job. Soon Amy's condo resembled a lush jungle hideaway, a welcoming haven after the pressure and bustle of her workday. Even her bedroom was transformed into a verdant retreat.

After one particularly wild day, when she'd grabbed a sandwich on the run for lunch and skipped dinner entirely, Amy put the key in her front-door lock at ten o'clock with a sigh of relief. To her surprise, the lock offered no resistance. The door was open and her Simon and Garfunkel record was on the stereo.

"Edith?" Amy couldn't believe the older woman was watering plants at night.

The voice that answered her didn't belong to her neighbor. "Edith went home to bed, but we had a nice talk." As Amy stood staring in amazement, Jack walked through the door opening out to the lanai.

"What . . . what—" Amy was shaking so much that she couldn't speak. She dropped her briefcase to the floor with a thud.

"We made ourselves a little snack, too, but I'll be damned if I could find any Cheez Whiz for the crackers. Oh, and I like your record. Played it a few times." Jack flopped down on Amy's couch and stretched his arm across the back. "She's a nice lady, Edith. I'd been sitting beside your front door for maybe two hours when she noticed me and asked me what I was up to."

Amy continued to gaze at Jack in disbelief. For the first time she noticed that an elaborate lei of large orchids rested on the glass top of her coffee table. Maybe she had been working too hard and was hallucinating.

"So I introduced myself," Jack continued, speaking as casually as if he'd just popped in from down the street. "Seems she'd heard my name a time or two." He glanced at Amy. "Edith decided you wouldn't mind too much if I waited inside, or I should say outside on the lanai. Nice view. You must be in the Oceanview Condos."

Completely dazed, Amy shook her head.

"No? Well, anyway, Edith kept me company until about half an hour ago, when the poor woman started dozing."

Slowly the numbness began to wear off, and Amy found her voice. "She . . . she never can last until the news. She always tries, but . . ." Amy shrugged.

"She's really cute, Amy."

"Yes, she is. And a wonderful gardener. She takes care of all my plants."

"She told me."

"I would have killed them off by now."

"She told me that, too."

"What . . . else did she say?"

Jack patted the flowered cushion next to him. "Come and sit down and I'll tell you."

Like a puppet on strings, Amy walked toward the couch and perched at the far end. She still half believed that if she got too close to him, this wonderful dream would end and she'd wake up in her bed alone, as she did every other time.

"You look like you've seen a ghost, Amy."

"Are you?"

"No. I'm the man who loves you, as I've mentioned a time or two before. And according to Edith, you're the woman who loves me."

"She said that?"

"Yes, and she chewed me out good for taking this long to show up. She thinks the world of you, Amy, and she had a hard time believing I was worth anything if I'd let you go."

Amy rubbed her forehead with a trembling hand. "And I'm having a hard time believing that you're here. I've been working long hours, Jack. I'm probably dreaming this, or seeing things."

"You're not. Come closer, Amy. I won't evaporate."

A whiff of his cologne reached her, and she wondered if people in dreams usually smelled good. She couldn't remember.

Jack picked up the lei from the coffee table. "I brought you this. Your old one was too dried up to make the trip. Let me put it on."

She gazed into the blue of his eyes as he slid closer and placed the lei over her head. "This will be the part where I wake up," she murmured.

"No." He touched her cheek. "I'm the one who had to wake up. I am the man who loves you, but I'm also your friend. Nobody said we couldn't play both sides of the record, Amy." He wove his fingers into her hair and his gaze searched hers. "If you'll forgive me for being such a jerk, I'd like to try it that way."

"I never blamed you," she murmured as his touch banished her last doubts that he was with her at last. "Your career is important, too. How could I ask you to change your plans if I wasn't willing to change mine?"

"You could because of exactly what you said. I'm more secure and established than you are. I can take the move much better."

"The move?"

"I've quit my job in Seattle. Tomorrow I'll apply for something here."

"You're moving to Honolulu?"

"Yep." He smiled. "I have to. My car's arriving soon."

Her eyes widened. "Your car's on its way?"

"Yep. And if it sinks in the drink, the bank will have my ass."

"I can't believe that you've already shipped your car."

"I took a chance that you meant what you said about living up to your word. A few months ago you may remember that you agreed to marry me."

Amy nodded as her heartbeat thundered in her ears.

"Are you a woman of your word, Amy Hobson?"

She ran her fingertips along the familiar curve of his jawline, and a sob rose in her throat. He had come to her. Jack was here, still wanting her, still loving her. She hadn't lost him. With a little cry of assent she hurled herself into his arms and clung to him while her tears soaked his shirt and the orchids crumpled between them.

He rocked her softly and smoothed her dark hair. "I'm so sorry," he whispered. "I've put you through so much."

Amy sniffed and looked up at him with brimming eyes. "That doesn't matter now. Nothing matters but being here together. I love you, Jack."

"You're probably a fool for loving me, just like Edith says, but I don't intend to talk you out of it." He smiled down at her and wiped the tears from her cheeks. "I'll try to be worthy of your love, Amy."

Amy's answering smile trembled. "Jack, are you ever going to stop apologizing and kiss me?"

Desire flamed in his blue eyes. "Consider the apologies over," he said hoarsely and lowered his lips to hers.

She matched the force of his kiss with a hunger even she hadn't known was there. They drew apart, gasping for breath, and gazed into each other's eyes.

Quivering with passion, she stood up and held out her hand. Silently he rose and followed her into the leafy bower of her bedroom. Each watched the other as they undressed by unspoken agreement. But when Amy hung the lei on a chair, Jack walked over and nestled it over her bare shoulders. Then, hand in hand, they walked to the bed.

Jack cradled her face in his hands. "So many lonely nights."

"But they're over now."

"Yes." His kiss was tender as he guided her to the soft sheets and covered her body with his, crushing the flowers between them.

The remembered sweet scent filled the room and ignited all the emotions Amy had kept hidden away for months. As she felt the friction of his chest and thighs and the press of his aroused manhood against her stomach, Amy grew dizzy with wanting him. "Now," she murmured breathlessly, opening her thighs. "I need you now."

He levered his body away slightly and gazed into her flushed face. "God, I love you," he whispered and thrust forward.

Amy dug her fingers into his hips and kept her gaze locked with his as she told him without words what he meant to her. And he answered in the primitive way that she understood, burying himself in her again and again until they both rocked with the convulsing power of their love for each other.

The lay together for long moments afterward. Pieces of the orchid garland were scattered about them like bits of lavender tissue paper.

At last Amy spoke. "Jack, can you really be happy here? I know Hawaii isn't where you want to live, but it may be a few years before I'm ready to move back to Washington."

He raised up on one elbow and looked at her with love shining in his eyes. "A few years of paradise? I think I can stand it."

"No, really, Jack. This isn't paradise for you."

He traced a path down the valley between her breasts. "I've learned something about paradise in the past few months."

"Have you?" She shivered with delight at his feathery caress.

"Yeah." He retraced his path and gently circled one taut nipple. "Paradise moves around."

"Is that so?"

"Um-hmm. Sometimes it's in one place—" he bent to kiss the puckered tip "—and sometimes in another." He moved to her other breast and bestowed a second kiss. "Finally I figured it out."

Desire pulsed through Amy once more. "Figured what out?"

"That paradise follows you around."

"Wrong, Jack." She pulled his head down until their lips were nearly touching. "It follows us."

Spoil yourself next month
with these four novels from

— TEMPTATION —

ON A WING AND A PRAYER by Jackie Weger

When Parnell Stillman's plane went down with Rebecca Hollis and five orphans on board, he had no intention of playing the hero. Being stranded with a bunch of kids and a wily woman made him a saint, or so he thought. Except a saint wouldn't be struggling with the temptation Rebecca put in his path.

LOVE LETTERS by Elise Title

As penpals, Alexandra and Greg had made a pact never to meet. But when the opportunity arose to see Greg, Alexandra couldn't resist. Only when he fell in love with the woman she was pretending to be did she realize the error of her charade.

OVER THE RAINBOW by Sandra Lee

After barely surviving a devastating tornado, Dana Cunningham swore she would never set foot in Oklahoma again. But twelve years later she was back home with the courage to face her demons. Or so she thought, until a storm sent her running into the arms of a total stranger.

THE PERFECT WOMAN by Libby Hall

Designer Kim Troussard never really hit it off with Sean Stevenson. He had always preferred a more traditionally feminine woman, definitely *not* one whose undeniably luscious body came complete with a rapier-sharp mind.

HOW FAR CAN LOVE BE CHALLENGED?

REDWOOD EMPIRE *By Elizabeth Lowell* £2.95
The best-selling author of *'Tell Me No Lies'*, creates a bitter triangle of love and hate amidst the majestic wilderness of America's Northwest empire. 19-year old Maya Charter's marriage to Hale Hawthorne is jeopardized by her lingering feelings for her former lover – his son, Will.

CHERISH THIS MOMENT *By Sandra Canfield* £2.75
Senator Cole Damon is Washington's most eligible bachelor, but his attraction to journalist Tracy Kent is hampered by her shocking past. If their love is to survive, he must first overcome her fear of betrayal.

BEYOND COMPARE *By Risa Kirk* £2.50
When T.V. presenters Dinah Blake and Neil Kerrigan meet to co-host a special programme, the only thing they have in common is their growing attraction for each other. Can they settle their differences, or is their conflict a recipe for disaster?

These three new titles will be out in bookshops from March 1989.

WRLDWIDE

Available from Boots, Martins, John Menzies, W.H. Smith, Woolworths and other paperback stockists.